# Winter LIGHT

CONNOR FALLS CHRISTMAS SERIES
NOVELLA

Robin Maderich

POTTER STREET BOOKS
ZIONSVILLE PA
2024

© 2014, 2024 Robin Maderich
All rights reserved.

ISBN: 979-8-9914596-4-8

Printed in the U.S.A.

Cover design by Robin Maderich

Potter Street Books/Robin Maderich Publishing
www.potterstreetbooks.com

This book is also available in digital format.

# Winter

## LIGHT

"I'm dreaming of a white Christmas…just like the ones I used to know."
— **Irving Berlin**

# AUTHOR'S NOTE

*Winter Light* is one of the novellas in the Connor Falls Christmas Collection, *When the Heart Brings You Home.* The three novellas are available separately as e-books, but I decided to have print editions prepared for sale only on my website. I know there are some of you out there who prefer to read your books on paper who would perhaps enjoy these special editions.

Happy reading everyone, and happy holidays.

Yours,

Robin Maderich

*Chapter One*

On her knees in the barren display window, Allie considered the challenge of vacant space. If nothing else, it could be a great topic for her next blog post. Her last had been on the most recent release in a young adult trilogy, the type of thing her customers had come to expect. They might not be so happy with a complaint about her inability to focus on this year's Christmas display. Thanksgiving had come and gone

and the four by eight foot area contained nothing but twinkling white lights affixed with tape along three sides. Blue painter's tape. She couldn't even muster the gumption to go out and purchase red duct tape from a hardware store that was no more than a five minute walk from the front door. Thank goodness her parents were in Florida. Even though they'd turned Connor Falls Book Emporium over to what they termed, perhaps facetiously, her 'capable hands', she was still answerable to them for the holiday receipts. Seasonal sales accounted for more than half the year's income. A window that was not only undecorated for Christmas but without any content whatsoever might put a teensy bit of a damper on customer enthusiasm.

Sunlight through the two huge windows gilded the recently swept hardwood flooring, highlighting its sterile condition. Shadows came and went across the surface as people passed by, no doubt wondering when Allie was going to get her act together. One shadow stopped and stayed. Allie looked up from contemplating disaster. A child's face was pressed against the window, handprints outlining her sleek, dark head like a smudged wreath.

The little girl's fingers curled into a fist. She rapped three times on the glass, the effect in the empty, echoing space like a series of small cannon blasts. Allie flinched.

"Don't do that!"

Seeing the child prepared to knock again, Allie lurched onto all fours and scrambled over to the window, crouching to get her face level with the little girl's. "I said, don't do that. Haven't you ever had a fish?"

"A fish?" the girl shouted back at her.

"Yes. A goldfish? In a fish bowl?  Never mind." Allie scanned the sidewalk. "Where are your parents?"

The girl jerked her still-fisted hand, thumb raised, toward the opposite side of the street. "My dad's at the bakery."

Allie frowned in the general direction of From the Hart bakery, the establishment owned by Gina Hart. People passed along the sidewalk, but none of them appeared to be searching for a small, dark-haired girl. Allie shook her head, wondering why a child who looked no older than six or seven had been permitted to wander across the main street and to the bookstore unaccompanied.

"My mom's in California. She lives there now."

"Entirely too much information to be shouting out to the world," Allie said.

"What?"

"Wait there. I'll be right out." Allie slid to the edge of the display space and hopped off, grabbing her coat from the stepstool. She headed to the front door with a shout over her shoulder to whichever employee might be within earshot that she'd be back in a few minutes. Outside, she found the little girl leaning with her back against the window, arms folded across her puffy, pink coat, fine dark hair blowing into her eyes. A backpack hanging off her shoulder pressed against the glass, revealing a doll sticking out the top and what looked like a potato chip bag clipped shut with a clothespin. Allie pushed her arms into her own jacket sleeves and zipped up. Her breath frosted in the air.

"Aren't you cold?"

The girl shook her head.

"Let's go find your dad," Allie said.

"No."

"Excuse me?"

"He knows where I am."

Allie tipped her head to the side, eyes narrowing. "He let you cross the street by yourself?"

The child tightened her grip across her narrow torso and glared at the sidewalk. Allie studied her defiant demeanor. She had a feeling the girl's father possessed no clue his daughter had wandered.

"What's your name?"

"Lydia," the girl said.

"Lydia. That's a nice name. Mine's Allie. And your dad's in Gina's bakery?"

Lydia glanced up from beneath frowning brows. "Who's Gina?"

"The woman who owns the bakery."

"Oh."

Allie looked again toward the bakery for a man in frantic search for a missing child. The people she saw striding from place to place appeared unconcerned, absorbed in their independent activities. Reaching down, Allie extracted Lydia's left hand from under her right arm and closed her fingers around the little girl's. "I can't be responsible for you outside my window and would feel guilty as all get out if you disappeared, so let's go find out what kind of goodies your dad's bought, shall we?"

Allie took three steps before Lydia pulled back on her hand, digging the heels of her pink rubber boots into the sidewalk. "I don't think I should go with you. You're a stranger. I think I should stay right here where my dad can find me."

Allie released Lydia's fingers. Lydia shoved her hand into her coat pocket as far as it would go.

"Well, you're right about that. I am a stranger.

Your dad really knows you're here?" That seemed irresponsible, allowing a child Lydia's age to wander freely about the streets, no matter how safe everyone viewed Connor Falls to be. "Can I call him for you, then? Do you know his cell phone number?"

"He doesn't have one," Lydia mumbled.

"He doesn't have a cell phone?"

Lydia shook her head.

"In this day and age?"

"He doesn't like that stuff."

"That seems odd," Allie said, more to herself than the child standing beside her.

"I'm not lying!"

Allie glanced down in surprise at Lydia's vehemence. "I didn't think you were." She studied Lydia's heart-shaped face a moment longer, noticing how the child avoided her eye, how her blue gaze focused earnestly across the street, but not at the bakery. A deeper suspicion settled in. "Lydia. Lydia, look at me, okay?"

The girl turned her whole body to Allie, her attention glued to Allie's denim-covered legs. Allie dropped to her knees, gazing up into Lydia's face. "Lydia, is there something you're not telling me?"

"What do you mean?" The girl's chin trembled, eyes welling up with moisture.

Despite herself, Allie's heart went out to her. She touched Lydia's arm. "Did you sneak away from your father? He could be very worried, you know. I would be."

"I…" Lydia hesitated, her mouth working. "He…he doesn't know where I am. I ran away from home, Allie. Daddy doesn't know where I am at all."

Curling her fingers over Lydia's sleeve, Allie drew her nearer. Huge, shining tears ran down the child's cheeks and dropped onto her coat. Allie inhaled, thinking hard. She'd run away herself a couple times in defiance of one restriction or another, but she'd never gotten very far before realizing her foolishness. She wondered how far Lydia had walked before coming to stop at the bookstore window.

"Where do you live?"

Lydia shook her head.

"You need to tell me. I'm sure your dad is scared."

"Scared?"

"Yes, scared. Because you're not there and he doesn't know where you've gone."

Lydia withdrew her hands from her pockets and wiped her face. Allie settled back on her heels to avoid the sidewalk chilling her knees through her jeans.

"Do you and your daddy live in one of the apartments above the stores?"

Lydia shook her head.

"A house on one of the side streets?"

Lips compressed, the child wagged her head again from side to side.

"Okay," said Allie, "I'll have to figure it out. Do you live in Paris, France?"

Lydia's chin jerked up. "What?"

"In a sunny little apartment on the Seine? Or perhaps in New York City? Just off Central Park?"

"Of course not." A reluctant giggle escaped Lydia's lips.

"Well, where then? Am I even close?"

Lydia shook her head so hard her hair circled out like a ballerina's tulle skirt. She gazed up at Allie, eyes wide. "Dad and I live in a place that used to be magic," she said, "but it isn't anymore."

Sadness pinched at Allie's chest. She remembered the days of magic, too. This child was way too young for enchantment to have left her life. "And where is that, sweetie? I really need to know."

Releasing a trembling breath, Lydia nodded. "Luke's Tree Farm. Do you know where that is?"

Of course Allie knew. Even if she had no other reason to know the farm, most everyone got their Christmas trees at Luke's, a huge place growing every

type of evergreen imaginable.

Nearly two miles outside of town.

"How on earth did you get here, Lydia?"

Lydia burst into tears.

*　　*　　*

Luke hung up the phone. He pushed his palm across his head, fingers dragging through disheveled hair.

"Damn it."

Snatching his coat from the rack by the door, Luke swore again. He shoved his arms into the garment, the fabric still chilled from his recent trek among the douglas firs. Pulling the truck keys from his pocket, he headed back outside to his pickup.

"Where're you going, boss?"

"Into town," Luke muttered as he yanked opened the pickup's door. He slid behind the wheel, pausing to take a steadying breath before turning the key in the ignition. It wouldn't do any good to go tearing along the roads like a lunatic. Lydia was safe with the woman from the bookstore. But how the hell had she gotten there? Normally, when Lydia got it into her head to take off, she headed up into the trees and he'd always find her in short order. This time, he hadn't even known she was gone.

"Lydia Hollis, you're going to be the death of me," he said as he put the truck into reverse and backed from the space in front of the house. Pausing before

heading for the long driveway, he rolled down the window. "Frank!"

The sandy-haired man ambled up to the truck. "Yeah, boss?"

"Is your wife still out of work?"

Frank's left brow twisted up toward his hairline. "Why are you asking?"

"Because I need some help with Lyddie. I can't keep an eye on her all the time. I thought I could, working around the farm, but apparently I'm an idiot."

"She take off again?"

Luke nodded.

"Sorry, Beth's back at work. Started last week at the hospital. That eight-year-old of yours is going to turn your hair gray. If she's this willful now, imagine what she'll be like as a teenager. My girls—"

"She wants her mother, Frank. And I don't know what to do about that."

As Luke drove the winding roads, he understood he could do nothing about Lydia wanting her mother. It was a frustrating, heartbreaking situation. Luke wasn't a fool. He'd consulted with professionals about what to do and basically received conflicting recommendations. Give her space; keep her close. Let her work through it in her own time; make her talk about the issue. The only thing consistent throughout was making certain Lydia knew he loved her. He thought he'd been doing that. Because he did. With his whole heart. Somehow, that wasn't enough.

Moving slowly through town, the main street decked out with wreaths and lights and bright flags for the holidays, he considered his own dark living room. Thanksgiving had come late this year. The business of selling Christmas trees was in full swing, giving him little time for anything else. Lydia loved Christmas. Once again, he'd let her down. After a brief and suitable punishment for her reckless behavior today, he'd make sure they broke out all the boxes filled with decorations and together they would do the house up right. The way it used to be.

Finding a parking space, Luke maneuvered the pickup into it and got out. He shut the door and took a deep breath, filling his lungs with crisp air, doing his best not to swear again as he thought of the distance he'd driven from the tree farm to Connor Falls. How had a little girl with legs the length of his arm managed to make it all that way without him noticing her absence? Safely, thank God, but even so.

Shoving his hands into his coat pockets, Luke marched toward Connor Falls Book Emporium. He hadn't been inside the bookstore in nearly two years.

Lydia used to love to come here, especially at Christmastime.

Luke paused outside the large display window, surprised to find it empty at this late date. Obviously, it had been cleared in preparation for decorating, but shouldn't that have been done days ago? He was a fine one to talk, with a little girl who loved Christmas and a house as bland and uninviting as a cardboard box. Luke strode up to the bookstore door and yanked it open.

"Dad!"

Lydia barreled into his legs. With a grunt, Luke scooped his daughter into his embrace and held her close, breathing in the scent of her hair before holding her out again at arm's length, her legs dangling. "Lyddie! Why did you run away again?"

As he spoke, he spotted powdered sugar on his daughter's lips. She swiped at her mouth with her knuckles. Luke set her on the floor.

"Lydia, I'm serious. What you did was dangerous. How did you get here?" He still couldn't believe she'd walked all the way into town, and yet he prayed she'd done exactly that, because the idea she might have managed to find someone to give her a ride, somebody without the sense they were born with, or worse, made his blood run cold. Lydia stared

up at him through shining, tear-filled eyes.

"I walked, Daddy. My legs hurt. And I'm sorry. I'm really sorry. Can we go home?"

Luke took a deep breath and slowly released the air through his nose. Maybe this was the problem. She always accepted immediate responsibility for her actions, and he couldn't bear her sadness. They'd developed a pattern that neither one could break.

"Lydia…"

"Daddy."

"You can't keep doing this. You could have been hurt, or gotten lost, or any number of things." Yes, things the town of Connor Falls, despite its reputation, couldn't guarantee wouldn't happen.

"But I didn't," Lydia said. "And I found a friend."

Luke frowned. "A friend?"

At the sound of a female clearing her throat, Luke glanced up from Lydia. Dressed in an oversized sweatshirt and jeans tucked into boots on slim legs, a woman stood behind his daughter. Her brown eyes gazed back at him from a small face framed by wispy, auburn curls. She looked vaguely familiar. He'd probably seen her around town, or picking up a tree. After giving him a quick onceover, she held out her hand.

"Hi. I'm Allie Roberts."

He grasped the hand in a brief shake. "Any relation to the Roberts who own the place?"

"They're my parents," she said. "They're semi-retired these days, so I'm running the bookstore now." She shrugged beneath the voluminous gray cotton of her shirt. "I bought Lydia a donut from the bakery. I hope you don't mind. I asked her first if she was allowed to eat sugar. You know, some parents are particular about that."

"It's not a problem," said Luke. "I appreciate you taking her in. I don't...I don't know what she's thinking, running off like this."

"Right here, Dad," said Lydia in a comical adult manner. Allie reached out and ruffled her hair. Luke's stomach flipped as if he'd dropped too fast in an elevator, the caress making him both sad and angry. Apparently, Lydia sensed his sudden mood shift, because she turned her head to gape up at Allie, blue eyes wide. Luke bent and grabbed Lydia's fingers in his own.

"Well, thank you again, Miss Roberts—"

"Allie. Please don't call me Miss Roberts."

"Yeah," said Lydia, "she likes Allie. Better than Allison, she told me."

Allie, better than Allison. The phrase struck him

with a brief flash of déjà vu. He couldn't imagine why. "Okay. Got it." He took a step backward toward the door. "And Lyddie, this is the final straw. I'm going to have to hire somebody to look after you. This is the busy season and I can't keep worrying that you're going to disappear. Do you understand me?"

Lydia hung her head, stealing a glance at Allie from beneath her bangs. "Allie said I could help her decorate the window."

"That was if I did it today," Allie explained. "As you can see, it's still empty. At this rate, Christmas will have come and gone and there'll be nothing in that window but dust."

"What's the problem?" Luke asked.

"I don't know. Even before my parents decided to back away from the business, I always did the displays. This year I wanted to come up with something really incredible, and instead my mind's a blank. I'm lacking inspiration, I guess."

"So's my dad," said Lydia. "You should see our house. Not one single decoration."

Luke bit the inside of his mouth. Yes, punishment, and then they would drag out the boxes and get to work.

"You could start with a tree," Lydia suggested.

"Do you have yours?" Allie asked.

"Not yet," Luke said. "You know the story of the shoemaker's family? That's me. But tonight. I promise," he said to Lydia. "And you come by, too, Allie. I'll give you a tree for the window, as a thank you."

"That's not necessary. I really didn't do anything."

"Yes, you did," said Luke. "I'm just grateful Lydia ended up with someone who looked after her. Stop by after dinner. We'll take flashlights and you can have your pick. I'll cut it down for you."

Allie hesitated. He wondered why. A free tree should appeal to anyone this time of year, especially somebody with an empty window three and a half weeks before Christmas.

"If you insist," she finally said.

"I do. So does Lyddie, don't you?"

"Yep," said his daughter. "And maybe tomorrow Dad can bring me here to give you a hand? I won't talk as much as I did today. I'll let you concentrate."

Allie laughed. The sound was shockingly infectious and, again, familiar. Smiling, Luke considered Allie more closely.

"Well, if you put it that way…" Allie jerked her head in the direction of the counter. "Don't forget your coat, Lydia."

ROBIN MADERICH

As Lydia skipped across the store to retrieve her garment, Luke hastened to nip the plans in the bud. He couldn't let Lydia inconvenience this stranger more than she had. "You don't have to do that. Really. I—"

"It's fine."

"But—"

"It's fine."

"It's just that she misses her mother so much."

"I know. She told me."

Luke's focus snapped from the antics his daughter was going through in putting on her coat back to Allie's face. His shoulders tensed. "What did she tell you, exactly?"

Allie tucked her hands into her pockets. "That her mother's in California. That she doesn't see her."

Luke compressed his lips, blowing a breath out his nose. His gaze strayed again to Lydia, still struggling into her coat beside the counter. He wondered if his daughter had said something more. He could tell by Allie's expression, though, that she hadn't.

"Okay," he said. "You come by tonight and pick a tree, and Lydia and I will deliver it tomorrow after you open."

"Deal," said Allie.

Lydia returned and Luke took her fingers. Striding to the door, he paused and looked back, the knob circled in his left hand and Lydia tugging on the other one. "I'm sorry. I didn't even introduce myself. I know we just spoke on the phone when you called, but I was a little agitated then. I feel like I've been rude. I'm Luke Hollis."

Allie met his gaze. "I remember exactly who you are," she said.

*Chapter Two*

Allie realized straightaway she should have just let him introduce himself and be done with it. Sometimes she didn't know when to leave well enough alone. She understood that, and yet she still managed to open her mouth and stick her foot in on a regular basis.

She watched his hand drop from the door knob. He bent and scooped his daughter up onto his hip, his expression caught between troubled and curious. Allie wanted to kick herself, or turn and walk away with a casual 'see you later', as if she hadn't said anything. Instead, she took a step closer.

"Have we met?" Luke asked.

"A long time ago."

"I…I don't remember."

"Yes," said Allie. "I can see that."

He stood silently in contemplation. Someone attempted to enter, bumping him in the elbow with the door.  He moved to the side, Lydia in his arms. The customer entered, easing past them both.

"When?"

"More than half a lifetime ago."

"So we were kids."

Allie nodded.

"It's no wonder I don't remember. I'm surprised you do."

"You kissed me." Damn it, why couldn't she just shut up?

Luke's eyes widened. He glanced down at Lydia, who looked both bewildered and amused. "Well, I—"

"It was no big deal."

"Obviously it was."

"No. It was a silly peck between two kids. It was what came after that made the incident significant."

His blue eyes narrowed. "What came after?"

She might as well get it over with, rip the bandage off with one quick pull, expose an old wound to the air. She'd forced the conversation and couldn't back down now. "I fell. On the ice on your father's pond. Broke my wrist."

"Broke your—oh."

"Yep," said Allie, as the skin on her cheeks heated up. He definitely remembered now. She could see memory blossom across his face. As a scrawny kid a couple of years ahead of her in school, he'd been awfully damned cute. As an adult, a father, a man grown into his own strength, he was handsome enough to make her stutter. Somehow, she'd been managing not to.

"I'm sorry," said Luke. "How could I have forgotten?"

"It wasn't quite as traumatic an experience for you," Allie said.

"Do you still skate?"

Allie faltered. "Oh. Sure. But I don't allow strange males to kiss me on the ice."

Luke threw back his head with a deep, rolling laugh. From the way Lydia looked at him, Allie figured he didn't do it often enough. He stopped, breathless from his amusement. "Did I know your name then?"

"I don't…I don't know."

"Wait. Sure I did. Allie, better than Allison. I knew that phrase sounded familiar."

The temperature in Allie's cheeks zoomed. "I really do have to get back to work, so…"

"I understand." He chuckled again. "We're leaving. Are you still stopping by later?"

"A free tree? I'd be crazy not to."

"Bye, Allie," called Lydia with a wave as the door closed behind them. Allie watched the two of them walk past the plate glass window, dark heads close together. Lydia twisted in her dad's arms, waving again like a participant in a parade. Allie lifted her hand in response, holding it aloft until they were out of sight.

"Why'd you tell him that?"

Allie jerked toward the sound of her employee's voice. "Don't you have work to do, Todd?"

"Yeah. And I was working right here. I heard the whole thing."

"He was bound to remember at some point,"

Allie said. "Better a preemptive strike before he did recall and I had to admit I'd never forgotten the incident, or lie. Either action would have been distinctly creepy."

Todd, eighteen years old and apparently blasé about matters creepy or otherwise, shrugged, lifting and placing the last book from the open cardboard box at his feet onto the display table. "So, once you get the tree, what are you going to do about the window? I don't ever remember you leaving it empty this long. People are going to start to wonder."

"Wonder what?"

"If we're open or closed."

"Good point," Allie said.

"I know. That's why I deserve a raise."

"Oh, hush, I'm trying to think."

"About what? That guy you kissed when you were fourteen?"

"How do you know how old I was?"

"Just a guess."

Allie surveyed the window again, twinkling lights reflecting off glass. "Well, I'm not thinking about him. I'm trying to figure out what to do with that blasted window. If worse comes to worse, I suppose I could recycle last year's idea."

"I wouldn't," Todd mumbled. He bent and picked

up the empty carton, tucking it under his arm. Tossing his shoulder-length, yellow hair away from his face, he set a tiny jingle bell dangling from the wire in his ear to tinkling.

"Why not?"

"Isn't that like wearing the same dress to a party two nights in a row? People tend to notice."

Allie laughed. "What would you know about that?"

"I have a sister."

Shaking her head vigorously, Allie left him and went to answer the ringing phone. On her way across the floor, she reflected on that long-ago kiss. Although it meant nothing to Luke, she'd been a fourteen-year-old with an awful crush on a boy who didn't even know her name. The kiss had caught her so off guard, she'd lost her balance and fallen on the ice, causing the night among her friends to go from something magical to an embarrassing—and painful—mess. Luke had managed to find her a few days later at school to ask how she was doing. After that, she avoided him and his circle of friends like the plague. He graduated later that year, solving her dilemma.

As she lifted the phone from the cradle, she thought perhaps Todd had been right. She really did need to keep her mouth shut. What point had there been in reminding Luke of the fool she'd made of herself? And now, she had to meet him in a few hours to pick out a tree, right near where the whole incident had taken place. It didn't matter how many years had passed since, because she'd been stupid enough to remind him. For crying out loud, she needed to carry a sock around to stuff in her mouth next time she opened it.

*  *  *

Lydia was unusually silent in the truck's passenger seat. Luke glanced at her several times, trying to gauge what she might be thinking. "Pumpkin—"

"Did you really kiss the bookstore lady?"

Crud. Was *that* what she was thinking about? "I did. We were very young."

"What about Mommy?"

"I hadn't even met your mommy yet."

"Oh."

Luke waited a few more minutes. "Does that bother you?"

"No…well, do you like her now?  Allie, I mean."

"I know who you mean, Lyddie. And I don't know her now. I didn't really know her then."

"But you kissed her."

"Well, yeah. She was wearing this white fluffy hat and her cheeks were pink and she skated like a pro." Good Lord, he couldn't believe he was having this conversation with his daughter. He put on the turn signal, concentrating on steering into the driveway, remembering suddenly that Allie had worn her unruly cinnamon hair long back then, and it had been braided down her back, tied with a thin, blue ribbon. Lydia remained silent beside him. "Sometimes teenage boys can be stupid like that," he said. "When you're a teenager, I want you to promise me you won't let any boy kiss you, okay?"

"Yuk," said Lydia, shooting a glance at him before she turned her gaze out the window. "I like Allie."

"That's good," Luke responded, uncertain where his daughter was headed with that comment.

"She told me she ran away once when she was little."

"Did she?"

"She ran away with her brother, so she said it wasn't as scary as being alone. She said they got as far as the bridge over Morgan Creek—do you know where that is, Dad?"

"I think so," he said.

"And then something bad almost happened to

them. She didn't say what it was, but she told me I must never, ever run away again."

Would that Lydia's behavior might actually cease on a word from a stranger. But he understood the issues behind it were too deeply entrenched to be rooted out by a simple story. Still, one could hope.

"She asked me where I thought I was going when I started out. I told her I didn't know. Why do I do that, Dad? I can't walk all the way to California. I know it's far away. And I don't want to. That would be stupid."

"Wanting to see your mother isn't stupid, honey," he said, reaching over to pat her hand. She let him for a moment and then pulled her fingers away, tucking them into her lap. She got like that, sometimes. Not wanting to be touched, as if she were afraid of being vulnerable.

"But she doesn't want to see me, does she?"

This was as close as Lyddie ever came to the pain she carried inside. Luke held his breath for a second. He knew he should be honest with his daughter, but he couldn't bear it. Besides, he didn't know the truth. Not really. Not enough to dash all hope. "Sure she does. Just give her time."

"What did I do?"

Anger colored Luke's vision for a moment as he

steered through people carrying wrapped trees to their cars. He headed toward the house. "Nothing, Lyddie. You did nothing wrong. If you don't believe anything else, believe that."

In silence, Lydia picked at a ball of lint on her coat. Even after Luke parked the truck, she continued to pluck her garment hem. Despite the topic between them and his daughter's withdrawal, Luke's thoughts were stirred by a vague optimism. He'd always been told things happened for a reason. Although Lydia's running away again, managing to make it into town, was both disheartening and frightening, maybe her ending up at the bookstore had been a blessing in disguise. She'd listened to Allie. Really listened, and spoke in her turn. Perhaps the wound had at last been exposed to a little healing balm.

*Chapter Three*

As she zipped up her coat, Allie reminded Todd to pull the a-frame sign from the sidewalk before he locked up. The newest books in their stock were listed on the sign. She'd decorated the corners with holly leaves and berries depicted in green and red chalk which had been scuffed off in certain sections. She really needed to break out the chalk and fix them. The pieces were right behind the counter in a coffee can.

What on earth was wrong with her?

"Off to see lover boy?" Todd asked from his position at the register.

Allie pointed at the sign, visible through the glass door. "Do me a favor and fix those holly leaves when you bring the sign in, will you?"

"Am I paid to be an artist or a clerk?"

Allie didn't answer. She yanked the door open and stepped outside, frowning at the lights framing the floor inside the window. They created a soft illumination of winter white, and if no one looked too carefully, they might believe something else existed inside the rectangle. Of course, if anyone came close to the window they would find only strings of bulbs taped along the boundaries of bare wood. Tomorrow, though, a live tree would be in the space. There'd better be a lot more than that before the morning was done. A complete display, in fact, or she'd be forced to give up and fall back on a bit of recycling.

Allie headed down the block in the direction of her car. Luke hadn't been too specific about the time she should come over, but she figured most normal people would have had dinner by now. With business picking up for the holidays, she ate her evening meal standing at the counter, usually just before closing. Fortunately, she had Todd and two others working tonight, allowing her the freedom to leave, but she hadn't eaten yet. As if reminded of the fact, her stomach gave a low growl. Eyeing the front of Gina's bakery covetously, Allie decided she would have something when she got home. No matter how delicious, a pastry did not constitute a solid meal.

Sliding behind the wheel of her car, Allie thought of Luke's brave but foolhardy daughter. Lydia was no doubt a handful for her father. He'd mentioned something when he'd come to pick her up about hiring help to look after her. Allie had no idea how long ago Lydia's mother had left, but it seemed Luke should have been seeking aid of some sort before now. Allie was in no position to offer any assistance herself, nor was she inclined to, since she barely knew the two of them, but she was looking forward to having Lydia in the store tomorrow. If nothing else, a pair of young eyes might be just the thing she needed for that stupid window.

Allie pulled the car from the parking space and headed out of town. She'd bought more than a few of her trees in the past from Luke's Tree Farm, but she'd always dealt with Luke, Sr. or one of his men. She'd heard in recent years that the younger Luke had taken over from his father. Maybe that was why she stopped going there and started buying pre-cut trees in the parking lot of the hardware store. She hadn't done it consciously, but now that she'd opened up to Luke about the incident on the pond, she realized she'd been avoiding him.

"Allie, you're an idiot," she said as she pushed her foot down on the accelerator, climbing the hill toward the sign in the distance. As she neared, she saw the driveway lined with lights leading to the red barn where the cut trees were brought to be wrapped for transport. A middle-aged man with sandy hair stepped out to pull a length of chain with a "closed" sign hanging from the center across the driveway. Allie stopped the car and rolled down the window. She leaned her head out. "Hi."

"Sorry, miss, we're closing for the evening. If you could come back tomorrow?"

Allie smiled, tipping her chin in the direction of a house on the hillside, windows glowing golden in the darkness. "I'm actually here to see Luke and his daughter. He told me to stop by. Is that his place up there?"

"Are you the one from the bookstore? Who found Lydia?"

"I didn't find Lydia. Lydia found me." She stuck her hand out the window. "Allie Roberts."

"Frank Mohr. Pleased to meet you. Yes, that's

Luke's place up there. His dad still lives in the house further down, but Luke built that one when he got hitched. Nice little place. A bit lonely for Lydia, though."

With a nod, Frank backed away to let her car through. Allie thanked him and proceeded to the point where the smaller drive veered off to the left and up the incline. Her stomach fluttered as she made the turn, exactly like the butterflies she used to experience in high school. High school? She still got them with inordinate frequency for a variety of reasons. Right now, it was if a kaleidoscope of the lovely creatures had taken residence in her gut.

It couldn't be because of Luke. It *couldn't* be. Not after all this time.

Biting her lip, Allie pulled up next to a pickup truck and parked her car. She sat for a full minute behind the wheel in silent debate before climbing out and shutting the door as quietly as possible. Hands shoved deep into her pockets, Allie made her way up a series of concrete steps to the lit porch, where she saw evidence of decorating in progress. Fir roping lay across the porch floor surrounded by strings of lights in various stages of disentanglement. A wreath hung on the front door. Allie spotted a Luke's Tree Farm tag dangling from the greenery. She reached up and

tucked the tag out of sight.

An oval of glass behind the wreath revealed an open, high-ceilinged room that combined living and eating, with the most beautiful kitchen at the far end. Seated at an island rather than the table, Lydia was engaged in consuming what appeared to be a grilled cheese sandwich. Luke stood beside her, the expression on his face a naked declaration of anxiety and awe and wrenching love as he turned to speak to his daughter. Allie took a hasty step back, not wanting to be an unwelcome witness to such honest emotion. As she did, she trod on a pair of pliers and sent them skittering against a metal table leg. She heard a shout from inside and looked up to see Lydia racing across the floor. The child yanked the door open.

"Allie!"

"Hi." Allie lifted her hand in greeting.

"Allie," said Luke, coming to stand behind his daughter, his fingers resting on her dark head.

"I'm sorry. I didn't realize you'd still be eating."

"We're running a little behind. I thought we'd get this porch done before dark, but…" He shrugged. "Come on in."

Allie stepped inside. Luke shut the door behind her.

"Lovely house," she said.

"Thanks. Lyddie, go finish your sandwich. I'll get my boots back on."

"I want to go, too." Lydia stopped mid-protest, mouth twisting. Allie figured she had to realize she was on thin ice. Making any demands after what had happened earlier in the day was not a good idea. "Please?" she said instead.

"Finish eating and we'll see."

Reluctantly, Lydia returned to the counter island, glancing back twice as she went. Defeated, she climbed up onto the stool and resumed eating.

Luke turned to Allie. He looked down. "What do you have on your feet?"

"I—what? I changed into my sneakers. I didn't want to muddy up my good boots."

"That won't do."

"Why?"

"Ground's way too wet out in the fields. Your feet will be soaked. Hold on, I'll be right back."

He walked toward the back of the house, leaving Allie standing in the living room. Allie did her best to act casual, studying the various photographs in simple black frames on the wall. They were quite good. She took a step closer to view the nearest group hanging to the right of the fireplace.

"My uncle Rory took all of those," Lydia said

from the kitchen. "He's a photographer. He has a book. You should carry it in your store."

Allie smiled, returning her gaze to the photos. She knew Rory Hollis was Luke's brother. She'd seen his work before and should have recognized it. "I'll check into ordering the book. I'd be happy to carry it."

"That's me and Mommy and Dad," said Lydia, nearer now. Allie turned to find the little girl standing on the opposite side of the long, gray sofa, the last of her sandwich in one hand, her other hand lifted and pointing. Allie followed the direction of Lydia's outstretched finger to a photo of a beautifully unguarded moment with Luke, a much younger Lydia and a brunette woman, laughing over something during dinner at the table in this very house. The lighting, the clarity, the particulars of position, amazed Allie. But something about the photo saddened her, too. After a moment, she understood what it was. Luke and Lydia were clearly attuned to the humor of the moment, but Lydia's mother, though possessing a broad smile, watched them both with a certain melancholy visible in her eyes.

Quickly, Allie rejected her conclusions. In the next instant, unmarked by the camera, Luke's wife had probably been laughing as openly as Luke and

Lydia.

Even so, the woman had left her family behind.

At the sound of footsteps, Allie turned her back on the wall of photos over the fireplace. Luke entered the room with a pair of old-fashioned galoshes in his hand. Allie forced her features into an innocent appearance, as if she hadn't been analyzing his life in the finite moment of a photograph.

"Lydia," he said, "if you're finished eating, put your plate in the dishwasher and go get your coat and boots."

As Lydia hastened to do as told, Luke continued across the room, coming to stand beside Allie. "My brother's an extremely talented man," he said, nodding toward the black and white photos. "That's my favorite. The big one in the middle."

Allie pivoted and moved to her left for a closer inspection. Rory had taken the photo from behind the two figures, the taller bending low, gloved hand hovering above his daughter's shoulder as they skated away from the lens across a frozen pond. Soft, diffuse illumination fell over them, around them, haunting in a way. Allie recognized the pond as the one outside Luke's dad's house, where she'd fallen. She refrained from comment.

"I can see why it's your favorite," she said. "The

image speaks volumes. They all do, really, but this one seems to epitomize the father-daughter relationship. Trust, guardianship, love, shared adventure. I'd say, based on the way she's holding her arms, that was one of Lydia's first times out on the ice?"

"Yes."

Allie glanced at Luke and away. He couldn't possibly be conscious of the unguarded, raw emotion on his face right then. Allie nodded at the photo. "The light is…I don't know what it is, except perfect."

"Winter light," said Luke.

"What's that?"

"Winter light. That's what Rory calls it. He loves to shoot when the air is cold and snow is pending and the world is without shadow and time seems held in abeyance. That's what he says, anyway. I can see what he means."

Allie looked up at the picture again. She could see it, too.

"Dad? Are you guys ready?"

Luke collected himself with a visible movement of his head, like a dog shaking rain from its coat. "Yep. Allie just has to put these galoshes on. Allie, you can slip your feet in, sneakers and all. That's what they're made for."

Allie sat on the edge of the sofa, reaching for the boots. The metal clasps had already been unfastened and she stuck her foot into the right boot, tugging it on. Her sneaker slid straight to the bottom in a nearly perfect fit. Not a pair of Luke's boots, then, and far too large for his daughter. Allie bit her lip. The symbolism of stepping into another woman's shoes wasn't lost on her. Neither was the ridiculousness of the sentiment. She certainly had no intention of becoming a part of Luke and Lydia's life. Not in that way. Not in any way. She didn't know either of them. Luke had been a one-sided high school crush, and Lydia…Lydia was a sweet child who had ended up at her store after an improbable trek to run from feelings she couldn't really escape. And that was that.

But things happened for a reason. Her mother said so all the time. Many people did, and believed it.

With a grunt of dismissal disguised as effort, Allie pulled on the left boot and rose. "Okay," she said. "Let's go find us a tree."

*   *   *

Luke strode in front of Allie, leading the way. Lydia had dropped back to walk with her and he could hear them chattering away behind him. He didn't want to feel what he was feeling, hopeful and interested. He had Lydia to think of. Part of what he was feeling had a great deal to do with her. She liked Allie, responded to her. But he couldn't base his attraction to a woman solely on Lydia. He really didn't have time for a woman in his life, anyway. Lyddie was enough to handle. And Allie was someone who happened to fall into their lives at a moment when she was needed. The fact he had kissed her once as a teenager was irrelevant. They were adults now, with their own pursuits and problems, grown far from the hormonal recklessness of adolescence.

"Where are we going, Dad?" Lydia called out.

"You'll see."

He had a plan, a plan that embarrassed him a little when it had come to him, but he was determined to see it through. Allie's reminder about the incident at his dad's pond had shaken loose other memories from that night. In particular, something she had said about the smell of balsam, how balsam and cinnamon were the scents of Christmas. Well, he couldn't do anything

about cinnamon right now, but a balsam tree in her window might be just the thing for inspiration. For some reason, balsam trees didn't do as well on the farm as other varieties, but he pampered a continual planting up on the ridge, for his own personal use. He didn't mind giving one up for Allie. She deserved it. He hadn't seen Lydia so talkative in ages.

Urging them on up the hillside with a wave of his flashlight, he smiled. In all honesty, he hadn't felt this good in a while either.

The scent drifted down on a breeze, reaching his flaring nostrils at the same instant it reached Allie's. He heard her gasp, a long, slow intake of breath, followed by a cry of delight. "Come on," he called over his shoulder. "We're almost there."

Lydia's boots pounded on the muddy pathway. She appeared beside him. He switched the flashlight to his other hand, the one holding the saw, and slipped his fingers around hers.

"Dad, are you sure?"

"Isn't it okay for Allie to have one of our special trees?"

"It's a great idea."

Luke smiled again. Allie scurried to catch up. For some reason, she hadn't fastened the boots and he could hear the rubber flapping around her calves as she neared and then passed him and Lydia, shuffling uphill with her arms wide.

"Fabulous!" she cried, spinning to face them. She stopped abruptly, arms dropping to her sides. Her eyes met his.

"Yes. I remembered," he confessed with a brief jerk of his shoulders. She bit her lip. "No big deal," he added, trying to stave off an emotion he couldn't handle. "It'll be nice in the window. Your store will smell like Christmas."

She fell in beside them in silence. They made their way up into the balsam grove. Lydia reached to take Allie's hand with her right one, but Allie had already shoved both of hers into her pockets and didn't see. Or if she did, she pretended not to. Walking hand in hand, all three of them, would have been strange. The fact Lydia wanted to created an ache in Luke's chest.

"I think there are some trees over this way that aren't too wide," Luke said, shining the light off to the left. In unison, they turned in that direction. Once there, Luke and Lydia stopped, although Allie plodded on in her unfastened boots for several seconds.

"Let's turn the flashlights off," said Lydia. "Just for a bit."

"Okay." Luke set the saw on the ground. "Ready? You, too, Allie. One. Two. Three."

He and Allie switched off their flashlights.

"Now look up," said Lydia.

Lydia stared up at the sky, her hair caught in her

ROBIN MADERICH

hood. Allie did the same, neck arched. Smiling, Luke turned his gaze skyward to a clear, velvet blackness filled with stars, some milky white, some yellow as topaz, others with the crystal brilliance of diamonds.

"Such a beautiful night."

Luke heard a catch in Allie's voice and cut his gaze sideways. In the star-filled darkness, he saw a glimmer of moisture in her eyes.

"Allie?"

"I'm fine."

He wanted to go to her, put his arms around her, but he understood she'd been moved to tears by natural beauty, not sadness. Besides, it wasn't his place to comfort her…was it? No, of course it wasn't. They were no more than strangers. Even on that long-ago night, he'd only known her by sight, not even her name, although she'd told him after she fell. They didn't travel in the same circles. She'd been at the party because she had friends who crossed those boundaries and she'd come with them. After watching her skate, he'd realized she hadn't cared about the party. She only wanted to fly across the ice beneath the night sky.

"Temperature's dropping. It's getting a little chilly out here." He bent and picked up the saw, flicking the flashlight back on. "Pick a tree, Allie.

Lydia, you can help her."

"And we can have hot chocolate after?" Lydia asked.

"Sure," said Luke. "If Allie has the time."

With the array of unexpected emotions battering at him, he hoped she wouldn't.

*Chapter Four*

Allie walked into the store and threw her purse and a shopping bag behind the counter. She turned on all the lights, unlocked the cash register, and performed a quick check of the displays to assure everything had been left in order at closing the night before. Satisfied, Allie jotted a quick note on a post-it to order Rory Hollis' book for the local author section, and then went to the display window. She

climbed inside.

Standing in the center of the barren floor, she turned in a slow circle. Her thoughts kept drifting to the evening before with Luke and Lydia. Although she tried not to let it affect her, she had been moved by the hike into the balsam copse. The fact he'd remembered a passing remark after all these years seemed significant, and yet she knew there was no way it could be. He happened to remember. Nothing more. The mind did funny things. The smell of a cup of tea could suddenly make you recall breakfast when you were four, for crying out loud. Luke's remembering meant nothing. However, the fact he'd brought her up to the copse once the memory had returned to him couldn't be so easily disregarded.

Even so, what did it mean? Only that he was kind, which she'd already deduced from his interaction with Lydia. Entertaining any other notion was a waste of time. She had to put this sort of nonsense out of her mind and focus on the project plaguing her. In about fifteen minutes Luke and Lydia would be here with the tree, and she didn't need to be mooning around. She needed to focus. She had a bag full of cinnamon sticks and red ribbon and her plan— her half-formulated plan—was to have Lydia tie ribbons to the cinnamon sticks. After, they would hang them on the tree. While Lydia did the tying, Allie hoped to finalize some masterful idea for the rest of the window, because really, she had none. Nada. Zip.

Catching sight through the glass of a wrapped tree balanced on a broad shoulder, Allie hurried to the edge of the display area and leaped to the carpeted floor below. She ran to the door and opened it as Luke appeared, stepping aside to let him in with the balsam fir. The scent of the tree filled her nostrils. He carried the tree to the window and laid it down, depositing a metal stand beside it. Allie looked outside for some sign of Lydia trailing behind.

"Where's Lyd—"

"She won't be coming," Luke said.

Allie made a face. "Is this her punishment for yesterday?"

"She doesn't know you. I don't think she would view not being able to come here as a punishment."

*Ouch.* "I was joking. And she was looking forward to coming here. I was looking forward to having her. But of course the decision about what she does with her day is yours."

"It is."

Allie's lifted her brows in disconcert. "Have I committed some mortal sin I don't know about? You

seem mighty miffed about something."

He turned from her and began to adjust the legs on the stand. She could gauge the depth of the breath he took in the expansion of his coat. After a moment, she heard the air release through his nose. He stared down at the stand, his hands at his sides.

"It's not you, Allie. I'm sorry. It's just…things are plenty screwed up right now. And Lydia is my problem, not yours."

"She's not your problem," Allie said quietly. "She's your daughter."

His head jerked as if he would make some sharp retort, but instead his shoulders slumped. "I know that. I can't have her pinning hopes on somebody who's going to be out of her life as quickly as she's come into it."

That sounded like a rejection to Allie. The little fantasies she'd been trying to quell all morning flittered away like birds escaped from a cage. "She's not pinning hopes. I liked her. She liked me. And she wanted to give me a hand. But I understand what you're saying, Luke. I do. If this is how you need to handle what's going on with Lydia, okay."

Whipping the tree to vertical, Luke lowered the stump into the stand and wordlessly tightened the bolts. He removed a small knife from his jeans and made short work of the wrapping. The freed branches descended gracefully into place. He still hadn't looked at her. "Once you set that where you want it, you need to get some water in the stand."

"Okay." Allie frowned at his profile.

"And you can just drop the stand outside the barn after the holidays."

"Okay." Allie tried to maintain a neutral tone. He had every right to keep his distance. There was no history between them. He wanted his life simple. She understood how that worked. And yet she felt a little like she'd been punched in the gut.

Luke pulled a couple of browned, curled maple leaves from impalement among the needles. He shoved them into his coat pocket along with the severed wrap, running his other hand through his hair. Allie crossed her arms over her chest. If he really wanted nothing to do with her—an impression she hadn't received last night—then why wasn't he leaving?

He pivoted on his rubber heel to face her. "Actually, Lydia isn't feeling well. I think all that time in the cold yesterday, all that unreasonable, scare-the-crap-out-of-me-to-even-think-about walking, must have run her down. She's in bed this morning. Frank—the guy you met out front last night?—called his wife over to sit with her until I get home, because my folks are out of town. I wanted to make sure you got your tree. And I know you're disappointed, because I can tell you really like Lydia—"

"Luke."

He took another deep breath, a shorter one this time, and waited.

"Luke." Ridiculously, tears pricked at her eyelids, clinging to the corners of her lashes. She blinked them back.

"Allie, don't—"

"Shh." She held up her hand. "It's fine. I'm fine. Ignore these," she said, waving her pointer finger at her eyes. "Makes no sense at all. A preposterous response. Compassion is my downfall. You carry enough responsibility. Don't feel responsible for my disappointment, too. You go on home to Lydia. And if you need anything, let me know. No strings, no expectations, no whatever the heck else you're worried about. Okay? Now that I've got a tree, I have a window to decorate."

He'd taken a step nearer. She hadn't seen him do it, hadn't noticed through her moist vision or her flurry of words. He wasn't the cute boy she remembered anymore. Not one bit. Instead he was older and careworn and marked by life to the point of impossible magnificence, and she wanted nothing more than for him to get out of her store right then, before she did or said another stupid thing.

"Did you find your marvelous inspiration?" he asked.

"Not yet."

"You will. I'll come by and check out the window with Lydia, when she's feeling better."

"Not necessary, Luke."

Pretending a nonchalance she knew didn't fool him, and which she certainly didn't feel, Allie clambered up into the window and started lugging the tree to a central position. She had to start somewhere, had to force herself to move in the right direction. More than that, she had to not look at Luke as he turned and left. She felt more than saw him pause at the glass, gazing in at her, and then he was gone. She stole a glance toward the street to be sure.

"You're an awful fool, Allison Roberts," she said, words echoing in the hollow space around her.

*　　*　　*

Luke gathered branches trimmed from the day's trees and carried them to the bin. Some places charged for greens, but Luke gave the fragrant castoffs to customers who asked for them, for wreaths or centerpieces or whatever they wanted. What they did with the castoffs wasn't up to him. He was glad to be rid of them without waste.

Frank had left early, so Luke pulled the chain across the driveway before heading up to the house. Lydia had been unusually quiet all day. Luke couldn't be sure if she still didn't feel well, was mad at him, disappointed, worried about the punishment for yesterday's antics that hadn't come, or what the deal was. After Beth had gone home, every time Luke checked on his daughter—and since Lydia had taken off the day before without him noticing, he made sure he did so with frequency—he found her sitting in her bed, reading or drawing. Their conversations went politely enough, but their interaction felt off.

Entering the house through the back door, Luke yanked off his boots and set them in the tray beneath the bench. The weather had definitely taken a turn, the temperature barely above freezing and the ground hard. His boots had been filthy last night after carrying the tree down from the hill with Lydia and Allie. Still bent over his knees, he looked at the two pairs of boots next to his, Lydia's bright pink ones and Zoe's old galoshes, left behind when she headed for her new life in sunny California. He pictured them on Allie's feet, flopping unfastened about her legs as she trudged along beside him and his daughter into the fragrant grove of balsam fir.

A guilty twinge unsettled him as he thought about his rudeness that morning. He didn't want to feel guilt, damn it. His fault, though. If he hadn't behaved like an ass, deliberately trying to put her off, he'd have no reason for self-reproach. She hadn't deserved that type of treatment. And when he'd tried to explain himself, she'd cried. Not because of hurt feelings, but because she felt *sorry* for him. He didn't want anyone feeling sorry for him, either, but especially not a kind, funny, and, yes, appealing woman. A woman he'd spent the day trying very hard to put out of his mind.

"Damn it," he said out loud, pushing up off the bench.

"Dad!"

Luke spun on the heel of his sock. "Lydia, what

are you doing out of bed?"

Her eyes widened. "Aren't I allowed to be now? You didn't say. Was I supposed to stay there until school tomorrow because I ran away?"

Reaching out, he pulled her close, ruffling her hair. "Of course not. That's not why you didn't come out, is it? I thought you weren't feeling well. Or were mad at me."

Lydia ducked her head away. "Do you think Allie did her window without me?"

Luke flinched as if he'd been hit by a flying dart. "I know she missed you being there, but she also needed to get the job finished, so I hope she did. Don't you?"

"I guess so."

Luke took her hand and led her into the kitchen. She sat on a stool at the island. Luke yanked open the refrigerator, searching for something to fix for their dinner. "Did you finish your homework?"

"I did that on Friday, Dad," Lydia answered behind him.

Luke sighed, lowering his head against the back of the arm hooked over the open refrigerator door. Of course she had. Lydia was a remarkable child...with the exception of the whole running

ROBIN MADERICH

away thing. But Luke understood that urge, too.

"Dad?"

"Yes, pumpkin?"

"Why don't we have Chinese? You've been working all day, and—"

"—and we can drive by Allie's store? Is that what you're trying for?" He lifted his head, looking back. Lydia sat with her hands clasped together on the counter, a beautiful, dark-haired angel. Not altogether innocent though. Her expression was anything but.

"Yep," she said. "I thought maybe we could take a look at the window."

"Get your shoes and your coat and my wallet off the dresser. You call, I'll buy."

Lydia giggled. "Of course you will. I don't have any money!" As she ran from the room, she shouted over her shoulder. "You want the usual?"

"The usual," he said and straightened. Before returning to the mud room for his shoes, he glanced in the small, ceramic-framed mirror on the wall, ducking from side to side in order to check his face for smudges of dirt. He smoothed his windblown hair with both hands.

"You're pathetic," he said. But the face looking

back at him was smiling.

Fifteen minutes later, snuggled in a pink coat that exactly matched the shade of her boots, a feat she had managed on her own the day he'd brought her shopping, Lydia watched him in the dimly lit interior of the truck as he steered the vehicle onto the narrow highway leading into town.

"You're not mad, are you, Dad?"

"Heck, no. I'm an adult and the word 'no' is in my vocabulary."

Lydia giggled, swiveling in her seat belt to face front. She had a fairly clear view of the road ahead. Luke could see her arching her neck for a better look. As soon as she spied the twenty miles per hour sign, she sat back, grinning.

"How long did they say before our order is done?" he asked.

"Just about now," she said. Disappointment tapped him on the shoulder. Despite his best intentions, he had found himself hoping Lydia's plans had included a stop by the bookstore, and not just a drive-by. "But don't worry," she added. "I ordered a large veggie rice for me, instead of the small one. I figured Allie might need something for her dinner."

Luke laughed and gave his daughter's tiny knee a squeeze. "You're probably right at that. Do you think she likes vegetable fried rice?"

"Who doesn't?"

It wasn't one of his personal favorites, but he had no intention of arguing the point with Lyddie. A short time later, he pulled the truck up in front of the restaurant.

"Can I come in with you, Dad?"

He nodded and they both got out. Inside, Lydia ran up to the box of fortune cookies and asked the fellow behind the counter if she could pick her own. She spent an inordinate amount of time in the process, her gloved hand hovering over the container, her eyes wide and intent as she concentrated on the wrapped cookies, hoping, Luke supposed, to choose the best fortunes.

"Come on, Lyddie."

"It's all right," said the man packing up their order. "Slow night."

Suddenly she pounced, plucking out three. She handed them up to be deposited into the bag with their food. Luke paid and they headed back outside and climbed into the truck. "So," he asked Lydia as he hooked her seatbelt, "did you pick out good

ones, do you think?"

"The best," she said with a grin.

"No, I picked the best."

"What do you mean?"

"I picked you."

She gave a very grownup snort through her nose. "You didn't pick me, Dad. I was born. That means I picked you."

Luke's heart swelled. "Good to know, sweetheart." He steered the truck in the direction of Allie's store. Within five minutes, he spotted a space big enough for the pickup and eased into it, giving his hair another quick glance in the mirror as he put the truck in park. One day soon, he should get it trimmed. He hadn't been giving his appearance much thought lately.

"Allie's not going to care about your hair, Dad."

He jumped, looking across the truck at his daughter. "What?"

"Trust me, she doesn't care about stuff like that."

"Really? What does she care about?"

"Who you are."

"Who I am?"

"Who all of us are."

Sometimes, the workings of his daughter's eight-year-old mind boggled him. She gathered information out of thin air and expressed very firm opinions about it. She couldn't really know something as profound as Allie's view of the people in her world. Could she? Could someone her age possess that type of intuition?

He thought of the rare occasions Lydia spoke about Zoe. His wife—ex-wife, he reminded himself—had left Pennsylvania over a year ago, making Lydia much younger at the time than her current, tender age of eight. Yet, the things that came out of Lyddie's mouth and out of the blue staggered him and made him bleed. A child shouldn't recognize such deep-seated truths about her parents. Not the ones that hurt so badly.

"Hand me the bag," Luke said, pointing. "We'll see if Allie finished the window or not."

The scents from the bag of Chinese food made his stomach growl as he stood on the sidewalk waiting for Lydia to climb out of the truck. As soon as her feet hit the ground, she placed her hand in his. A day would come, impossibly soon, when she wouldn't reach for his hand like that anymore.

Swallowing hard, he forced a smile to his lips.

Nearing Connor Falls Book Emporium, Luke spotted a handful of people standing in front of the display window, pointing and talking. Lydia noticed as well, tugging him forward.

"Oh, Daddy," she whispered as they came to a halt before the window.

Luke stared, too, feeling his face go numb and then hot. He shook his head once, very slowly.

How Allie had managed all of this in one day, he couldn't imagine. The tree and about a dozen books provided the only color in a display that had been made to resemble a black and white photograph. The light from a multitude of tiny white bulbs behind gauze draped along the ceiling illuminated the scene with a gentle glow, revealing a landscape recreated in varying shades of off-white and gray. A pond in the center—made from foil sprayed with a mist of white paint—reflected the light from above softly. Logs had been coated white with a dry brush to tone down their natural hue, and against one lying vertically in the fake snow beside the pond leaned a pair of old, white ice skates, the cracked leather highlighted by a skillful application of some type of dark gray glaze. At the nearest edge of the pond was positioned a large silhouette of two figures skating cautiously onto the ice, the hand of the taller hovering just above the shoulder of the child.

"Is that us?" Lydia asked, still whispering.

"I think it's meant to be every parent and child," Luke said. His gaze shifted to a sign made to resemble a scroll, affixed to a small post in the snow just to the right of the figures. Written on the parchment-like paper with a calligraphy pen, were the words:

"The radiance of winter comes from within, seeping out from our hearts to illuminate each day and light our way back to precious memories."

Below it in neat block letters was a request for people to bring in gray-scale copies of photographs of their favorite winter memories, to be hung on the tree. No photos hung on the branches, but the sign couldn't have been up more than a few hours.

"Isn't it lovely?" said a woman standing next to him.

He nodded, once again speechless. The woman moved away and someone else took her place.

"Hey, Lydia. Feeling better?"

Luke spun on his heel. A dusting of glitter

sparkled in Allie's short, cinnamon hair. She raised her gaze from Lydia's face to his. Had he ever really forgotten how luminous her chocolate-brown eyes could be?

Pulling her close and crushing the bag of food between them, he kissed her in a way he never would have done all those years ago.

*Chapter Five*

Allie pulled away first, breathless, the pounding of her heart momentarily drowning out the sounds in the street.

"Uh, hi," she finally managed.

Luke stared at her, apparently horrified by what he'd done. Beside him, Lydia looked up at her father with annoyance.

"Dad, I think you broke the fortune cookies." She

yanked a bag from her father's fist. "Come on, Allie," she then said to her. "We brought Chinese!"

Taking her hand, Lydia led her into the store and up to the counter. "Hi, Todd," the girl said as she marched around behind. "There's enough for you, too, I think."

Todd winked at her. "Don't worry about it. I just had a hoagie." His head lifted, looking over Allie's shoulder. With a hasty nod, he excused himself. Allie turned around.

"I'm sorry," Luke said. "I don't—I'm sorry."

Allie could hear the crinkling of brown paper as Lydia rummaged through the bag out of sight behind the L-shaped counter. Allie kept her eyes fixed on Luke's as she fought the curling of her lips and the churning of her stomach.

"Those were the exact words you used sixteen years ago. Right down to the little hesitation between 'I don't' and the second 'I'm sorry'. What were you going to say? Then and now, I guess. 'I don't know what came over me'?"

"No," he said, "I know exactly what came over me. Then and now. And I am sorry."

Allie cocked her head to the side, pondering Luke's expression. She couldn't get a clear picture of the workings of his mind right then. It didn't appear to be regret. Not entirely. She suspected an inclination to run lurking there somewhere. She tossed her head. "For what? A momentary urge? Forget about it. I'm more intrigued by why you brought me Chinese."

She turned away, suppressing her own impulse to grab him by the front of his coat and kiss him again. Too late, anyway. Lydia had popped up from behind the counter to deposit food containers on the surface.

"Dad, what's wrong with you? So you kissed Allie. Big people do that all the time. I've seen it on TV."

Unable to stop the giggle bubbling over her lips, Allie headed to the back office for a couple of paper plates and napkins. When she returned, she found Lydia had doffed her coat and climbed up onto the tall stool, but Luke hadn't moved. "Luke, it's all right," she said, looking at him as she handed Lydia the plates. "I swear you haven't scarred me for life or anything."

He said nothing.

"Come. Eat. I can hear your stomach rumbling from here."

"Allie…"

At his tone, she set the napkins down and turned. "Luke. Seriously. It's okay."

The troubled expression in his blue eyes said otherwise. "Allie, can I talk to you a moment? In private."

Allie hesitated. She took a deep breath, releasing it in increments. Her stomach flipped nervously. "Lydia, man the store. We'll be right back."

"What if someone wants to buy a book?" Lydia asked, straightening on the stool.

"Call Todd. He's good at that. We're only stepping out front. We'll be back in before the food gets cold." Allie signaled to Todd before she headed for the door. And on the off chance she had underestimated the time it would take for Luke's discussion about why there would never be anything between the two of them, Allie grabbed her coat.

Outside, Allie strode away from the display window to a patch of sidewalk not as well lit. She wasn't certain she wanted him to see her face with any clarity during this conversation. When she ascertained they'd reached a point where he

ROBIN MADERICH

couldn't, she stopped, shoving her hands into the pockets of her coat.

"Allie, I…look, I don't know that Lydia's ready to handle something like this."

Allie turned her head slightly, looking at him from the corner of her eye. "Like what, exactly?"

"Like me…dating."

"Dating? We're not. I mean, you haven't said a word to me about it. No, how'd you like to go to the movies, or…well, you get the gist."

"Well no, but—"

"Were you considering asking me on a date? Frankly, I figured you kissed me to see if it felt the same now that we're both grown up, relatively speaking."

He laughed and shook his head. Some of the color came back into his face. She hadn't realized how pale he'd become until then. She knew, though, that she'd never had that affect on anyone else in her life.

"I like you, Allie. I don't know you that well, but that's usually how it works. You feel a liking for someone, or an attraction, or whatever it is that moves you, and then you do your best to get to know that person. Right?"

Allie bit her lip. This wasn't going at all in the direction she'd expected.

"That kiss should have come later. This one, not the one years ago. I don't remember exactly how I felt about that one. I'm betting I liked it just as much, though."

Allie's mouth dropped open. She sucked in a small amount of cold air.

"But what I'm saying is anything I choose to do must be done with consideration for Lydia. She's my daughter, and she's already hurting."

"Understood." Allie could barely get the word out.

"Because Lydia likes you, too. If things don't work out between two people, kids get caught in the middle."

"Stop," said Allie. "You don't—"

"Yes, I do. I want to get to know you better, Allie, but I want to take things slowly. Oh, God, I'm not even giving you a chance to say what you think. Have I just stuck my foot in my mouth?"

Allie released a breath through her nose. "I have a permanent toe print on my tongue from doing that. And no, you haven't. If you want to ask me out, go ahead and do it. My answer will be yes."

His lips lifted in a slow smile. He leaned forward and pressed his mouth to her forehead, whispering against the curve of her brow. "Perfect."

*   *   *

Luke scrubbed his hand across his eyes, blinking them tiredly. Remnants of his leftover sweet and sour chicken spotted the plate at his elbow, the fork on a crumpled napkin nearby. He glanced at the clock. After midnight. He and Lydia had spent more time at the bookstore than he'd intended, leaving him to start his paperwork for the day far later than usual. But he'd finished and he had the memory of a pleasant evening to ease him into sleep.

Capping the pen and closing the record book, Luke then rose and scraped his plate into the trash can. He'd been working in the light thrown from the stove hood so as not to disturb Lyddie, who'd fallen asleep on the sofa, and it pooled around him, leaving the rest of the area in near darkness. Even so, the light glittered in the glass of the picture frames above the fireplace mantel. Careful not to disturb Lydia, he moved to the photo of the two of them on the ice and stood staring at the image, his arms crossed over his chest. The silhouette Allie had made was not, of course, an exact duplicate of him and Lydia, but she'd definitely managed to recreate the mood. Although she had spoken enthusiastically about Rory's talent, she possessed an artistic ability of her own.

Taking a step back, Luke viewed the other photographs on the wall. Each of them contained at least one family member, and yet none of them were portraits. Rory used people in his photos as another element of his art, yet distinctly personal. Luke didn't quite get how Rory managed to make that happen. Luke didn't possess a creative bone in his body, but he recognized the attribute when he saw it.

At a sound from the sofa behind him, Luke turned. Lydia had rolled in her sleep, the blanket he'd covered her with slipping to the floor. He went to pick it up, pausing at the sight of a slim piece of paper sticking out between Lydia's fingers. Crouching down, he slid the paper out of her hand and held it up to the light filtering in from the kitchen, recognizing a fortune from one of the broken cookies in the bag. Lydia's fortune, he figured, since both he and Allie had laughed over theirs but Lydia had never read hers out loud, interrupted by a bookstore customer coming to the counter.

He looked closely at it now, experiencing a small dread as he realized the words were important to her, something she wanted to believe in, or she never would have held onto the fortune through the entirety of the night. He'd done the same thing himself as a kid, and even, he had to admit, as an adult, but Lydia's wants and wishes were so often wrapped up in the bigger drama of their lives.

*Your dreams really can come true.*

Harmless enough, but he remembered the way she'd agonized over the picking of the cookies. She counted on this fortune. And he knew what she dreamed about, heard her talking often enough in her sleep.

Luke inserted the fortune back into her hand, closing her fingers around it. He picked her up and carried her to her bed, lowering Lyddie onto the mussed mattress and pulling the covers over her. He kissed her softly on the brow and straightened, staring down a moment at his sleeping, troubled daughter. With an expulsion of breath from his

nose, he returned to the kitchen, grabbed his phone and dialed.

Standing in the yellow light from the stove hood, Luke listened to the ring, preparing in his head the message he would leave. Instead, she picked up, throwing him, causing him to hesitate.

"Hello?"

Luke cleared his throat. "Zoe, it's me."

*Chapter Six*

Keys in hand, Allie paused by the display window, studying it with a critical eye. Customers had been telling her the past few days how much they liked it, and yet not one of them had come forward with a photo for the tree. For that matter, neither had she. Perhaps they felt as underwhelmed with the season this year as she did. She only wanted it to be over. And why was that, precisely?

"Allie, hi!"

Allie turned, spotting Gina waving from across the street. Figuring it wouldn't kill anyone if she opened a couple of minutes late, Allie waved back and, after a quick check for non-existent traffic at that hour, hurried over to talk to her.

"Are you just getting in?" Allie asked, eying the bakery door. Nope, the sign was already flipped to *OPEN*.

"I stepped out for some air. Beautiful morning." The dark-haired woman smiled. "How are you doing? Love the window."

Allie shrugged. "Thanks. I'm surprised I managed to come up with any idea at all, because I'm not feeling it this year."

"Some years are like that. You don't quite manage the ho-ho-ho bit."

"You, too?"

"No, surprisingly, I'm good. I hired a baker to help me, which has made a world of difference to the stress I experience as the holidays approach."

Nodding, Allie checked the sidewalk in front of the Book Emporium to make sure no one was looking to get in.

"So what's this rumor I hear about you and the hot Luke Hollis?"

Allie jerked back around. "As opposed to the not-hot Luke Hollis? Does that man exist?"

Gina snorted a quick laugh.

"Where did you hear this rumor? Because that's all it is."

"Todd," Gina said. "And what do you mean that's all it is?"

"He expressed an interest and I haven't heard from him since." Allie shoved her hands into her jacket pockets, jiggling the shop keys around. "And that's fine. He has his daughter to think of, the tree farm. We're all busy now."

"Apparently, he's managed a bit of time for you."

"He—what?" Allie followed Gina's gaze and spotted Luke's pickup pulling the wrong way into a vacant space near the entrance to the bookstore. With a rushed goodbye, Allie hurried across the street. Luke lowered the passenger side window. Allie draped her arms across the opening, leaning her weight against the door. "Hi."

"Good morning." He grinned. Somehow, it didn't reach his eyes.

"Whatcha doing?"

"I came to buy a book."

"I'm not open yet."

"I can see that."

"What kind of book?"

"Something for Lyddie," he said. "She's had a rough couple of days."

Allie backed away, fishing the keys from her pocket. She jerked her head in invitation and went to unlock the knob. The solid slam of the truck door sounded behind her. "Let me get the lights on," she said.

He followed her inside, waiting in the middle of the floor as she hurried to the bank of switches.

"What's happened? Has Lydia been sick, or…?"

"I called Zoe after we left here the other night. Actually got her on the phone." He shoved his hands into his pockets, rocking back on his heels. "I wanted to know…to know how she could do this to our daughter. I've asked before and her answers have always been, well, crap. This time I kind of lost it. I got loud. Lydia woke up. She heard…me. The things I was saying. She asked to talk to her mother and I put her on the phone. How could I not? She rarely gets to speak with Zoe and I thought, okay, I've said my piece, you're her mother, Zoe, you explain it to her."

"And did she?"

"Yeah, unfortunately I think she did."

Allie flicked the last switch, lighting the area over the register. "Not good?"

"I don't even know what she said. I tried to listen, but she'd gotten quiet on the other end and Lydia's responses soon became monosyllabic. Until the end. She asked Zoe if she'd come home for Christmas to see her. To see…to see us."

Allie observed the play of pain crossing Luke's face with a wrench to her gut.

"Zoe didn't answer the phone when I called back. And Lyddie wouldn't say a word. She cried herself to sleep. She didn't want me to touch her. I let her sleep in and brought her to school late." He sighed. "She's not good, and I don't know what to do to help her now."

"Does she have—"

"A therapist? Yes. I took her. Don't know if it helped."

"And your wife—"

"Ex-wife."

"Zoe," Allie amended. "What exactly is she doing in California?"

"Following her dream." His sarcasm was obvious.

Allie remembered the stunning good looks of the woman in the photographs on Luke's living room wall. "Acting?"

"I suppose."

Luke had been right. This wasn't the time to start a relationship. He had too much on his plate, too much upheaval and anguish and unresolved issues for that. Even so, Allie wanted to put her arms around him, hold him close. He would always be there to comfort his daughter, but who comforted him?

"What kind of book were you thinking? Something to entertain, distract, console, commiserate? What's her reading level?"

She headed for the children's section, Luke on her heels.

"The school advisor says she's well ahead of her grade level in reading."

Allie nodded. "That doesn't surprise me. Let's look around and you tell me if you recognize any of the books as something she's read recently, and that'll give me something to go on."

She crouched on the floor, pulling a few middle grade readers from the shelf and holding them up to Luke.

He knelt beside her. "This one. And this one. She read that twice, she told me."

With a smile, Allie yanked several more down, spreading them out on the floor by her knees. She placed her fingers flat on the nearest. "I'd try this."

His hand lowered onto hers. "Thank you, Allie."

She nodded in mute acknowledgment, afraid to speak. His tone moved her to the verge of tears. After a moment, she eased her hand from beneath his and rose, clearing her throat. He picked the books up from the floor and returned them to the shelf, then took the one she'd suggested from her grasp.

"You're right. I think she'll like this one."

His eyes had such beautiful form, almond shaped and long-lashed. The color reminded her of the sky in the last light of day. She gazed into them for longer than she intended. He didn't look away.

"Allie."

"Don't kiss me again."

"Ever?"

"Right now I don't want you confusing gratitude with affection."

"Give me a little credit, Allison Roberts."

She growled at him and marched to the front of the store, where she reached under the counter and grabbed a bag. She deposited the book into it when he gave it to her. "Here you go, Luke. If you don't think it'll upset her, please tell Lydia I said hello."

"I'm paying you for this book."

"Nope. It takes ten minutes for this old register to warm up, and I don't think you feel like waiting."

"Liar."

"Maybe."

"Look, Allie, you can tell her hello yourself. She'd probably like to hear from you. I don't think it would harm her to have a conversation. In fact, she talked about you before she got on the school bus this morning."

Allie placed her elbows on the counter, leaning toward him. "What did she say?"

"She said…" He swallowed. "She said, 'you like Allie and Mommy's never coming back, so you should ask her out.' What eight-year-old says things like that, let alone thinks them? What have Zoe and I done to this wonderful child of ours?"

His heart suddenly lay in her hands. She closed her eyes. She hadn't been looking for this either, not something so complicated and heartbreaking. Still, she couldn't back away. He needed…something. A friend, a willing ear, someone to tell him he'd been doing his best. She lifted her lids and gave him a long, weighty look.

"Lydia hurts, Luke, but she's not broken. You haven't broken her. She's sweet and super-smart and, yes, extremely introspective for an eight-year-old—heck, I don't think I'm that introspective—but you love her, and she knows that. And that's important. I hate to play devil's advocate, but I think Zoe loves her, too. How could she abruptly stop? Maybe she avoids contact because it's painful to her and painful to Lydia and she doesn't know what else to do. She could be just as confused as you, having made a decision to follow her dreams, as you said, and knowing Lydia would be better here with her dad, in a stable environment." Allie straightened, turned the register key. She shrugged. "I don't know. I'm just a bookseller with no kids of my own. I see a lot of them, though, and Lydia is a special little girl."

Luke stared. After a moment, he backed away from the counter. "If Zoe had expressed even half of her motivation, it would have helped. I don't know what she's thinking. Once I thought I understood her." He shook the bag in his hand. "Thanks, Allie, for the book and…everything."

He left. No promising goodbye. Just gone. The door opened thirty seconds later. Todd walked in.

"Hey, isn't that your old crush pulling away?"

Allie blew a breath out her nose. "Yeah."

Todd shirked out of his coat and hung it on the rack. "So, you guys got plans, or what?"

"More like 'what'."

"Oh, jeez, I'm sorry." He headed into the back room to put his lunch in the refrigerator. Allie opened the register and slipped a ten from her pocket into the

proper bin. Connor Falls Book Emporium was still her parents' establishment and she had no business handing out merchandise without payment. She'd get the bar code later, ring up the book and settle the till.

"I brought you a picture for the tree."

Allie turned to see what Todd was holding out. Frowning, she took the photo from his hand. "What is this?"

"You wanted a favorite winter memory. This is me and my buddies playing paintball a few winters back. Those balls were *frozen*. They hurt. I had bruises after. But we had fun. It was one of the best, last days I had with Cyril." He tapped the picture above the head of a boy standing beside him, tall and lanky and dark. "He was killed a week later in a car accident."

Allie's fingers shook. "Oh God, Todd."

"Hey, Allie, don't be crying. It's all right. He was my best friend for years. We had that time. Some people, they don't find a friend like that. How much worse would my life have been if I never had him?" He reached past her for the hole punch and ribbon she'd brought in with the expectation of photos to be hung, then removed the picture from her grasp. "I'll hang it myself, if that's okay?"

"Yes," Allie managed to croak. "Hang it up high.

That's something to be proud of."

"And maybe it'll get other people thinking. You haven't asked them for the impossible. Just to share something of themselves."

Perspective. Everything was a matter of perspective. Todd's raw, honest sentiments burned into her heart. If only she had managed to say something so profound to Luke, she could have helped him.

The front door opened again, this time admitting a customer. Allie put her game face on, smiling at Jeanette Nolan as she walked up to the counter. If the woman noticed her still-wet lashes, she made no comment. "Hi, Allie. I've come for my package. How are your folks doing?"

"Enjoying Florida. Your family? Are they coming for Christmas?" Allie retrieved Jeanette's package from beneath the counter and scanned the codes from the three books into the register.

"All except Eve. You know."

Allie did know. She recognized the disappointment in Jeanette's voice each year. Allie swiped the woman's credit card and returned the books to the bag. "My parents are staying in Florida for the holidays and my brother is with his wife's family this year. I guess you have to get used to that

sort of thing."

Jeanette eyebrows wiggled in dubious agreement as she reached for the bag Allie extended across the counter. "What's this I hear about you and Luke Hollis?"

Good Lord, this town wasn't *that* small. Catching the wink Jeanette sent in Todd's direction, Allie understood exactly where the woman had received her information. "There's nothing going on between me and Luke, Mrs. Nolan. We haven't even had a date."

As she spoke those words, Allie felt a little like she wanted to run and hide. After she fired Todd Wilkins.

*Chapter Seven*

Luke's strides took him swiftly to the bottom of the driveway to meet Lydia's bus. Since Lydia's conversation with her mother, he'd been careful not to be late. Part of him only wanted to show Lydia he was there for her, always. The other part feared she'd disappear somewhere between the road and home and this time she wouldn't be found.

The squash-colored bus pulled to a stop, lights

flashing. The door opened. For a heart-thudding instant, no child appeared. And then there she was, her coat open, the plaid dress and striped tights she'd insisted on wearing this morning endearingly quirky. He'd learned not to argue with her about her attire, except as it related to weather. She was a third-grader with her own style.

She waved to someone inside and then leaped down the steps, throwing her arms out once her booted feet landed on the ground. Luke stepped forward and scooped her up onto his hip. "How was school, pumpkin?"

"We made stuff."

"What kind of stuff?"

"Secret stuff. Presents. I made one for you, and one for Allie."

Luke's stomach fluttered. "Allie?"

"Yep. And Grandma and Grandpa."

Luke waited. When she didn't go on, he asked, "And Mom? Did you make something for her?"

Lydia's expression turned solemn. "I did. I made her a special card. When everything is dry and I bring it home, we'll put it in the mail." She wriggled down to stand beside him. She slipped her hand into his. "It's cold out today."

ROBIN MADERICH

"That's why you should have your coat zipped up."

"It was warm in the bus. Do you think it will snow?"

"Not yet, sweetie."

"How about the pond? Is it frozen yet?"

"Nope. Why?"

"I thought we could go skating again. Like in the picture."

Like in the picture. Lydia had skated a lot since Rory took the photograph, had learned to do so quite well. But Luke knew what she meant. There'd been something extra special about that day. Maybe because it was her first time and everything was new, to both of them. He hadn't taken his daughter skating before that moment. She'd always watched him from her perch on a pond-side log, sitting beside her mother, or she'd scoot around on the soles of her boots at the frozen water's edge. Zoe didn't skate. Claimed to be a klutz on the ice. And, in all honesty, she was. Her legs went in all directions like a newborn foal. She probably would have killed herself if he'd forced her out there. And he never had.

"Dad? You okay?"

"Yep. Just thinking about things. You might get your wish about the pond. An arctic front is supposed to be dipping down low by next week. You think you're cold now? You wait. You're going to need your hat and mittens and everything."

Lydia let out a whoop. "Cool!"

"Cool?"

"Yeah. My friend Edgie says that all the time."

Luke smiled. Must be a new girl. "Edgie? What kind of name is Edgie?"

Lydia shrugged. "I dunno. Hers?"

Laughing, Luke whipped the backpack off his daughter's shoulders. He tucked her football style beneath his arm and took off at a trot up the driveway with Lydia's high-pitched screams of joy warning customers out of their way.

*　　*　　*

"What's wrong, boss?"

Allie glanced up from the catalogue of spring releases to meet Todd's eye. "Besides the fact you've been blabbing tidbits of my personal life around town?"

"Yeah. Besides that."

Closing the catalogue, Allie inhaled, trying not to crack a smile. She failed, snorting through her nose before breaking into laughter. "You're an idiot, Todd. Why, why, why would you think it was okay to talk about me to people?"

"It came up. People asked how you were doing. They couldn't fail to notice how long it took you to do that window, after all, so they figured something was up."

"Right. And the reason you brought up Luke?"

He arched his brows with an 'are you kidding' kind of look. "They were all female. Naturally, they assumed your problem was the lack of a guy in your life."

"Oh, for crying out loud." Allie stormed out from behind the counter and grabbed her jacket. "I'm going to take a walk. It's slow right now. Want me to bring you something back?"

"From where?"

"I have no idea."

She exited the store into temperatures far cooler than they'd been a couple of hours earlier. The sun was nearly down, the street dark with winter shadow and streetlights glowing against the dimming sky. Windows up and down the block

twinkled merrily. Allie breathed the crisp air, trying to clear her head as she made a right on the sidewalk, walking past the window without looking at it. She didn't want a reminder how she had failed to inspire the townspeople with her bid for Christmas memories. Maybe no one was in the mood this year. Except for Todd, with his jingle bell earring—knowing what the photo he'd hung on the tree meant to him touched her deeply.

Turning her collar up, Allie continued along the block, gaze glued to the place in front of her moving feet. She thrust her hands into her pockets, shoulders hunched against the chill of her thoughts as much as the dropping temperature of evening. People spoke to her and she nodded and smiled in automatic greeting, not lingering to chat. She had no destination in mind, except perhaps a rapid walk around the block and back inside again. Instead, she found herself crossing the intersection and striding up to Hannah's department store. She paused on the busy sidewalk, her eyes on the name carved long ago into the stone block of the building in old-fashioned lettering. She'd been coming to this store all her life, with her brother and parents as a child and later as an adult. Even though a shopping mall existed less than a half an hour away, it was to Hannah's she came first. Same with the bookstore. People patronized Connor Falls Book Emporium to purchase a physical book, rather than traveling to the huge conglomerate store or ordering online, and she was grateful to them for that. For the most part, Connor Falls' residents were long-term inhabitants who prided themselves on shopping locally. If not for their dedication, many of the icons of the community might have succumbed to the flagging economy.

Allie laughed out loud, causing a couple of folks to turn her way with uncertain smiles. She was beginning to sound exactly like her father—at least in her inner thoughts. Scary.

Wending her way closer to the nearest window, Allie came to a halt in front of it. She studied the display with the same critical eye she used on her own, considering the yards and yards of fake snow, the huge, fake tree hung with brilliant balls, the oversized alphabet blocks, the wrapped gift boxes and, of course, particular items of interest displayed in the open ones. After a moment she took a single step back to view it as a whole, and not with the goal of comparison or judgment. Recalling how she

used to look forward to the display every year as a child, running up to the glass and smudging it with her fingers in the same manner Lydia had smeared the plate glass of her undecorated window almost a week ago. In that instant, the old, remembered magic whipped through her like a flame and even though it only lasted an instant—that nostalgic joy of anticipation and wonder—the aftereffect remained warm in her heart.

"Looking for more inspiration?"

Allie refocused her gaze onto the reflection in the glass beside her where a tall, handsome man held the hand of a small, dark-haired girl beside him. "Nah," she said. "Just looking. It's lovely, isn't it?"

"It's magical," Lydia said. Allie smiled.

"Not that yours isn't," Luke hastened to add.

Allie winked at Lydia in the glass. "It's like being a kid again."

"I am a kid."

"I know," Allie said, "but I'm not. At least, I'm not supposed to be. But I think a big part of me still is."

"There's nothing wrong with being a kid. Is there, Dad?"

"Nope," said Luke, smiling at Allie in the glass. "Not at all."

Allie met his gaze with a smile of her own before turning around to face them both. "What are you two doing? Something fun?"

Luke raised his hand and shook the bag clasped in his fingers. "Lights. To replace those I had. They're about ten years old anyway—before they started making strands that don't go out if only one bulb has blown. We'll save figuring out which one went for a summer project."

"That could be entertaining," Allie said. "Plugging in the Christmas lights in July."

Lydia tugged on her father's hand, pulling him away from the window. "Will you help us, Allie?"

Allie cocked her head at Lydia. "What? In July?"

"No, tonight, silly."

"I—" Allie glanced at Luke, then back down at Lydia. "I have to go back to the bookstore. Todd only lets me out for five minutes at a time."

"Todd's not your boss," Lydia announced in a long, slow drawl.

"I know. I'm teasing. But not about having to get back to work. I really do."

"Long days. You open and close?" Luke asked.

"During the holidays, yeah. Usually."

"How about after? It's Friday, so Lyddie gets to stay up late. We could watch a movie."

"With popcorn?" Lydia piped.

"With popcorn," Luke agreed. "Allie? What do you say?"

Allie searched Luke's eyes. "Are you sure?"

"We all have to live our lives. Yes, I'm sure."

*　　*　　*

Allie cut out early, leaving Todd to close the store once again. She really did need to give him a raise. He deserved one. Possibly the position of assistant manager, too. Not that there was an actual manager. She didn't have a title, but it would mean a lot to him to be officially called something and she could successfully argue the increase in salary when it came time to explain her decision to her parents.

She stopped at the bakery and bought half a dozen cookies. Seemed reasonable. Two each. Not an exorbitant amount of sugar at this hour. Besides, Gina's pumpkin-spice cookies were to die for.

When Allie arrived at Luke's home, the strands of white lights had been placed around the door and windows, as well as a set of what she presumed were battery-operated twinkle lights wrapped around the wreath. Gray wisps rose from the chimney against the night sky, seasoning the air with the scent of burning logs. Centered in the living room window a decorated tree sparkled behind glass. All the gaiety reminded her she hadn't gotten a single decoration in place at home. She didn't usually do a lot, but she liked a tree. It almost seemed a waste to get one this late.

Allie approached the door, the box of cookies tucked under her arm. She'd flossed, brushed and gargled with mouthwash in the bathroom at the store. Couldn't do anything about her clothes, though, short of going home, which would have taken way too much time. Besides, this wasn't a date. Not a romantic-type date. This was—this was what? A friendly evening, the three of them. She wouldn't think of it as anything more.

Lydia yanked the door open before Allie had the opportunity to knock. The varied scents of their earlier dinner wafted out along with the evergreen's fragrance. "Come on in! We're watching Sleeping

Beauty!" With a squeal, Lydia rushed back toward the couch and leaped onto a cushion. She yanked a blanket off the arm and wrapped it around her body.

Allie stepped inside and closed the door. Luke appeared beside her.

"It's her favorite."

"Works for me," Allie said, handing him the box of cookies.

Although the couch would have held the three of them with room to spare, Allie shirked out of her coat and took the deep, soft chair next to the sofa. "Do you need help with anything?"

"Just grabbing the popcorn and we'll be set. Something to drink?"

"Do you have any type of cola? Although I don't usually indulge in caffeine at this hour, I don't want to fall asleep before the prince gets his girl."

Luke's deep, rich chuckle brought an irrational blush to her cheeks. Fortunately, he handed her the glass of soda without looking at her, then took his seat beside his daughter. He placed a heaping bowl of popcorn on the coffee table. "Lyddie, slide over closer to me so Allie can sit on the sofa with us. It'll be easier for her to reach the popcorn."

Self-consciously, Allie moved to the last cushion and sat, crossing her legs. A few seconds later she uncrossed them and reached for a handful of popcorn. The dvd had already been positioned in the player and after Allie reclined against the chair back, Luke hit *play*. She could sense his eyes on her. She tried to ignore him, but before long cut her eyes in his direction.

"Relax," he said. "And try to stay awake. I like when the prince gets the girl, too."

He tossed a purple throw in her direction. She snatched it from the air and spread it over her legs. The flames on the hearth made the room cozy, but the blanket seemed to be part of the ritual. Luke had one, too, which he balanced still folded on his knees once he stretched his long legs out, feet on the table. Lydia glanced up at her father, finger on her lips, before laying her head on a pillow on Luke's thigh. In a breathless falsetto, she hummed the brief opening refrain of "When You Wish Upon A Star" and settled down as the movie began.

Allie wondered what Todd would think if he could see her now, what he would impart to the ladies when they asked again after her emotional

state. Not that it mattered. But she might give him a little fuel for his discussions. She might tell him she was happy.

*Chapter Eight*

Luke waited until the credits had rolled to their conclusion before moving his leg. Lyddie didn't make a sound, not even a mumble of protest. He stood and gathered her into his arms together with blanket, pillow and the stuffed rabbit she'd insisted they stop the movie in order for her to find. On the opposite end of the couch Allie slept draped across the arm, the blanket he'd given her tumbled around her feet on the floor. Up until a couple of minutes ago she'd been snoring like a puppy. He'd never tell her. At least not anytime soon.

Luke carried his daughter into her bedroom and tucked her into bed, waiting to be certain she wouldn't waken prior to his return to the living room. Lately, he'd been leaving the nightlight on. He'd heard mixed comments on that one, but he didn't care. She slept better with it on and the pennies in electricity weren't going to break him.

Allie didn't waken upon his approach. He eyed the couch, considering whether he could scoot her up onto the cushions, cover her up and leave her there, but decided things could get very weird very quickly if he did that. Besides the fact they hardly knew each other, he understood how disoriented she would be if she woke up here.

Crouching on his left knee near the couch, he looked at her. He really did like her short hair, so different from the long mass of curls of her teenaged years. Those had been attractive, too, but the flyaway, pixie strands framing her face these days had a definite appeal. He studied the shape of her eyes behind their closed lids, her long, reddish brown lashes, the freckles bridging her nose. He could kiss her awake like the prince in Sleeping Beauty, but

she'd have every right to smack him if he did.

"Allie."

She didn't stir.

"Allison Roberts." He touched a strand of hair on her cheek, pushing it back.

Her eyes flew open, staring blankly ahead before focusing on him. With a gasp, she sat up and wiped her mouth with the back of her hand, blinking several times. "I'm sorry, Luke," she mumbled. "Some guest I am."

"It's all right. I expect you were tired." In fact, it was more than all right. Falling asleep like that meant she'd finally relaxed. And he wanted her to be comfortable around him, around the two of them, him and Lyddie, because he wanted Allie to come back again and again.

"What time is it?" She glanced aside at the empty couch. "Lydia's gone to bed?"

"She was sound asleep, too. I just carried her in."

She nodded, yawning. "So what time is it?"

"I don't know. Around ten-thirty, I think."

"So my secret is out. This is how I spend my Friday nights this time of year, passed out cold before ten."

He didn't want to tell her he'd had two late cups of coffee to make sure he didn't do the same. He

stood, extending his hand. "Here, let me help you up. The bathroom's through there. You might want to splash your face, wake yourself up a bit. And you're perfectly welcome to stay here, if you're too tired to drive. As you've discovered, this couch is pretty comfy."

Standing beside him, she yawned again with a shake of her head. "I don't think I should."

"Your call. There are two cookies left. I'll heat up some water for tea and we'll eat them before you go."

She smiled, sleepy and amused. He imagined she might look like that most mornings and then dismissed the vision in his head, going to the kitchen to fill the teapot as she headed for the bathroom.

Five minutes later she returned, looking more awake, the hair around her face slightly damp. The kettle was coming to a boil and Luke quickly cut the flame beneath before the pot whistled and woke up Lydia. "Better?"

Allie took a seat at the island. "Better."

He poured steaming water into two mugs and gave her one, taking the seat next to her. "Some date, huh?"

She giggled. "Was that what it was?"

"Well, until the holidays are over, I think that's going to be the extent."

Allie lifted her mug and inhaled. Steam wafted toward her nostrils, no doubt fragrant with the tea bag floating in the water. "So, you still want to do this,

then?"

"I still want to do this."

Her lips turned up, eyes crinkling at the corners. She took a sip of tea. He leaned in, planting a kiss on her temple.

"I like you, Allie. Lydia likes you. Which is, of course, my major concern, if things don't, well…you know."

"I know." Allie picked up one of the cookies and bit into it, chewing with an expression of mild euphoria. "Gina makes the best bakery cookies."

"It might have been better if Lydia hadn't met you, didn't know you, because I could keep this part of my life separate from family life."

Allie took another bite, talking around it. "But if she hadn't met me, it's not likely you and I would have run into each other again, is it?"

"And you wouldn't have confessed to kissing me."

"You kissed me, Luke Hollis."

"That I did." He kissed her again, on the corner of her mouth, catching a cookie crumb on his tongue from her lip. "I tried to talk to you after, but you avoided me."

"I was embarrassed."

"So was I. I couldn't believe I'd been such a jerk and you'd broken your wrist because of it."

She waved the hand clutching the half-eaten cookie. "Still works, so no harm done."

"And do you still skate, Allie-better-than-Allison?"

Setting her mug down, she turned to look at him, her wide eyes reflecting the overhead light. "No."

The muscles in his abdomen tightened in response to that single word. He couldn't help remembering again the way she moved on the ice, graceful and at ease, arms fluid, legs engaged in effortless maneuvering, as if she didn't have to give a single thought to what her body needed to do to propel itself across the slick frozen surface. "Not because of—"

"No. Goodness, no. I…I just ran out of time for that." She appeared bewildered by the admission. Luke removed the cookie from her left hand and slipped his fingers around her own.

"Let's do it together then. Lyddie wants to go out on the pond, too, but I think the first time it should be just you and me. Like a real date."

She frowned. "Tonight?"

Luke laughed, swiftly stifling the loud noise and lowering his voice. "The pond's not frozen yet, but with the trough of arctic air moving in, it should be soon enough. Once the pond is solid, that'll be our first, real date. Deal?"

She grinned and nodded. "Deal."

Luke pushed back the stool and stood. "I'm thinking before another long day, you might want to head home and get some sleep. Are you okay to drive?"

"Perfectly."

He retrieved her coat and held it out for her to put on. She clamped the remains of the cookie between her teeth and slipped her arms into the sleeves of the garment. He zipped it up for her, fingers lingering at her chin. "I'll walk you out."

Outside, their breath mingled in a clouded dance. He'd come out without a jacket and hunched into himself against the frigid temperatures as they kissed goodnight. Overhead the stars stood out in brilliant clarity.

"Sunday is early closing, isn't it?" he called after her as she headed for her car.

She turned, walking backwards. "It is, but I have extra people on the weekends anyway, so I could leave a little early. Why?"

"Come back and have dinner. I'll make something special."

She stopped walking. "You cook? Well, of course you do." Her laughter filled the silence of the night. "I'll see you Sunday then."

Luke watched Allie's car until it was out of sight. He stood a moment longer, listening to the fading sound of the engine until that, too, was gone. As he headed inside, he told himself everything would be all right.

*     *     *

"Thank you, Mrs. Brennan." Allie waved at the woman as she left the shop, and then took the photo she had supplied and climbed into the window to attach it with a ribbon to the tree.

"How many is that now?" Todd asked. "Counting mine."

Allie looked the tree over. "Counting yours? Nine."

"Nine? Are you kidding me?"

"Nope. Maybe people don't have as many fond memories as I'd hoped."

"Or they're just too busy to hunt them up. Like somebody else I know."

Allie jumped from the window to the floor, hastening to grab the nearest display to stop it from wobbling. "I need to go over to my parents and look through the old photo albums. And yes, I haven't had the time."

"Right. What about tonight? You're leaving early."

"Did I tell you I was making you assistant manager? I think I've had a change of heart."

"You can't do that. I'm sure there are laws against such a thing."

"I'm sure there aren't." Allie returned to her place behind the counter. "But I wouldn't dream of taking back your promotion. You've done a good job for me."

Todd said nothing, staring at her with his hands on his hips.

"What?"

"Are you in love with your old crush?"

Allie frowned, blindly rearranging a stack of brochures on the counter. "Are you saying you think my business decisions have been based on my love life, such as it is?"

"No. I'm just wondering if you're happy." Sticking his hands in his pockets, Todd sauntered toward the back of the store, calling over his shoulder. "Don't forget the pie in the fridge before you leave."

Right. The pie. She'd "made" a pie instead of buying one, a tasty treat she'd loved as a kid and figured Lydia would enjoy as well—chocolate pudding in a graham cracker crust. Not very grown up, but what the heck. After talking with Luke twice, he still hadn't told her what he was making, so she couldn't show up with something that might complement dinner. Apparently, he wanted to surprise her. As soon as Bridget returned from her evening meal to man the store with Todd, Allie would head over to Luke's. If she got there early enough, she could lend a hand with the preparations.

*　　*　　*

"Set the table, Lyddie."

When he didn't receive an answer, Luke turned from stirring the simmering contents of the pot on the burner to see where she'd gone.  She stood exactly where he'd seen her last, staring at him.

"We're eating at the table?"

"Of course we're eating at the table. Allie's company. When Nana and Poppy come to eat, don't we sit at the table? Can't use the counter all the time, sweetie."

He saw her eyes shift a little and knew she was trying not to look at the framed photo by the fireplace of the three of them—him, Lydia, Zoe—at the table. He'd seen her looking at it before, many times. Always her gaze drifted to her mother. He wondered if she saw what he did in that picture, or if her young mind sought and found something entirely different. Something she wanted. Something she needed to see.

But no, Lydia saw the truth like no other. It was her gift and the core of her heartache.

"Do you think she'll come for Christmas, Dad?"

He knew she didn't mean Allie. Letting a breath out, he crossed the floor and crouched down in front of his daughter. "I don't know."

"We'll call though, right?"

"If you'd like." So seldom did Lydia receive an answer when she called her mother's number, though, it wasn't likely she'd reach Zoe on Christmas either, especially since he still didn't know what had transpired during the last mother-daughter conversation. "I'm sure she'll be waiting to hear from you on Christmas," he lied, rising, touching Lydia's hair in passing. "We'll sing her a song on the phone, how's that? Think of a good one."

"Jingle Bells. We used to sing it together, remember?"

Compressing his lips, Luke nodded and went back to the stove. "Set the table, Lydia. I'm putting the water on to boil now."

As Lydia took the dishes off the counter and distributed them around the table, Luke filled the pot at the sink, thinking about Allie. Was he making a mistake, beginning a relationship with her when so much remained unresolved in his life? In Lydia's?

"Do you like her, Dad?"

"Your mom?" he asked, wanting so much not to have to answer that question.

"No, silly. Allie."

Luke set the pot on the stove and closed his eyes. "Yes."

"I do, too. It's not wrong, is it, Dad?"

"Of course it isn't. We like many people in the course of our lives."

"But we don't love them all. What happens when they don't love us back?"

Ah, Lydia and her uncannily direct and un-childlike questions. "It hurts and we learn to live with it." At Lydia's lack of response, Luke turned from the stove, discovering his eight-year-old in silent, adult tears. He rushed to her across the floor, gathering her up against his chest. She threw her thin arms around his neck.

"Oh, pumpkin, I'm so sorry."

She hugged him tight. "Mommy hurt you, too, didn't she?"

"We're grown-ups. It's different."

"I want to be grown up, Daddy. I want to be grown up now."

*Oh, no you don't, Lyddie. You stay young for as long as you can, because even though the greatest hurts are there, that's also where you'll find the deepest magic.* He kissed the side of her head, the fine, dark hairs tickling his nose. At a tentative knock on the door, Luke carried his weeping daughter over to answer it. If Allie was going to be in their lives, she would have to get used to the occasional drama.

When he opened the door, though, Allie wasn't

standing on the other side.

*    *    *

Allie turned up the long driveway to Luke's. He'd left the chain down and coiled to the side in anticipation of her arrival. In the passenger seat of her car, the pie sat with a wad of tissues beneath one edge to keep it level. She'd driven carefully to avoid stopping short and ending up with chocolate pudding plastered across her glove box. As she neared the front of the house she saw the Christmas lights lit once again and a vehicle next to Luke's truck. Maybe his parents had stopped by. After she parked and climbed out, pie balanced across her palm and a quick hip-check to shut the driver's side door, she realized by the plates on the other car that it was a rental. She glanced up at the house. The front door stood wide open.

She climbed with hesitant steps to the porch, pausing at the door to knock on the jamb. The overhead lights in the kitchen illuminated a meal in the making, steam rising from a huge pot, plates on the table, a variety of dishes and utensils on the counter. At a noise like the sniffling of a contained sob, Allie leaned forward to peer into a living room lit only by the lights on the Christmas tree and the glow of the kitchen fixture. Near the fireless hearth Luke stood with Lydia in his arms, both of them embraced by the stunning woman from the photographs, and all of them crying.

Zoe had come home.

## *Chapter Nine*

Dazed, Allie slapped her hand across the coffee table's surface, seeking her phone. She'd had the foresight to set the alarm, but not to put the damned thing where she could reach it. Figuring she might need extra incentive for rising, she'd also chosen the most annoying tone. And now, of course, it wouldn't stop.

Allie swung her legs from the sofa cushions and

sat up, squinting in the early light. Locating the phone, she grabbed the device and turned the alarm off. Her gaze strayed to the empty pie plate and soiled fork lying in a gob of chocolate pudding beside it on the coffee table. Vaguely, she remembered finishing off the remains of the two-day old pie last night. No wonder she felt sick.

She closed her eyes at the memory of sneaking away from Luke's open front door to her car like a thief in the night. When she'd pulled from the parking space and looked forward again, she'd found Luke standing in the driveway inches from the car's hood.

*Allie, I'll call you.*

It was all right. She understood. At least, she told anyone who asked her—since apparently everyone within her circle of friends, acquaintances and customers had somehow gotten wind of Zoe's return, as well as Allie's tentative involvement with Luke— that she understood. The logical, mature portion of her brain did recognize without doubt the importance of a child reunited with her mother. The other part, the part that was perhaps still fourteen years old, couldn't help but dwell on the image of Luke weeping in the arms of his ex-wife and the fact his words *I'll call you* were the last she'd heard from him.

"Oh stop being an idiot. You're going to be late

for work."

Late, she couldn't be. Today what she called her 'last hurrah shipment' was due and she wanted to make sure the books received were displayed to the best advantage. After that, she had plenty of other things to take care of. Really, this time of the year wasn't the most opportune for starting a relationship anyway. She had more things to do than she had hours in the day. Look at her house. Not a single decoration in place. Tonight when she got home, that would be exactly the task for her—yanking out boxes and placing the contents in all the traditional places around the cottage. It would look like Christmas in here whether she liked it or not.

With a sigh, Allie gathered up the mess from the coffee table and dropped it in the kitchen sink, then went upstairs to dress for her day.

*    *    *

Luke hoisted the wrapped tree into Sheila Jefferson's open trunk. He watched her pull down the driveway and waved as she reached the bottom. Fortunately, the woman didn't have far to drive with the tree sticking out like that.

"It's cold out here."

Luke glanced aside at his ex-wife. "Yep. It tends to do that in December. In Pennsylvania, anyway. What's it like in California?" He shoved his hands into his pockets. A strange sort of day, weather-wise. Damp and chilly, but he couldn't tell if snow was in the offing or rain. Zoe touched his arm. His whole body went stiff.

"What time does Lydia get home?"

"Same time as yesterday. Same time as last year. Three-forty-five."

"Are you angry with me, Luke?"

Luke turned to look at her. She tossed her head, long, shiny brown hair drifting over the shoulder of a rather insubstantial jacket. "I am, Zoe. How can I not be? I don't need you any more in my life, but Lyddie does. And you…you haven't been there."

She slipped her hand into his pocket, burrowing her curled fingers into his palm. "I could stay. I could stay if you want me to."

"Don't make this about us, Zoe. Don't waste your time and mine." Luke stepped away. Zoe's hand dropped to her thigh. Zoe was one of the few women he knew who stood nearly eye to eye with him. He couldn't imagine where Lydia's diminutive height came from. His mother's side probably.

Strange thing, genetics.

"What are you thinking about?"

Luke hunched his shoulders beneath his coat. "Nothing."

"I'd like us to try. Why couldn't we try?"

"I have an extra coat hanging in the mudroom. Why don't you put it on, so you don't freeze while you're waiting for Lydia's bus?"

"See?" She backed away from him with her hands in the rear pockets of her dark jeans. "You do still care."

Luke blew a long breath over his lips and headed toward the barn. There, he picked up the cast off greens and threw them in the bin. Frank observed him from a short distance. Luke deliberately ignored the man's expression.

"You all right, boss?"

"Fine."

"You don't look fine."

"I said—"

"In fact, you look mighty troubled. It's that wife of yours, isn't it?"

"Ex-wife, Frank." At the sound of the bus pulling up, Luke turned his attention to the road. Zoe stood at the end of the driveway, a faraway,

narrow figure swimming in his coat, arms wrapped around the waist to cinch it in as she waited for the doors to open. When they did, Lydia bounded out and straight into her mother's embrace. Luke's heart contracted. For so long, even before Zoe headed west to California, it had been him and Lyddie, day in and day out. He didn't know what to do with the strange, sudden emptiness in him.

"Lydia's happy to have her mom back," Frank said beside him.

"Zoe wants to work things out."

"Between the two of you?"

"That's the gist."

"And?"

"I don't want any part of that." This time, though, Luke would be the bad guy if Zoe left again. Lydia would blame him for not taking Zoe back into their lives. Because his gut told him that would be the way it would play out. All or nothing.

Turning on his heel, he snatched up a log from the ground, tossing it as he spun. The wood landed in the bin with a shuddering bang. Apologizing to Frank, Luke stormed off up the hill into the evergreens.

Lydia found him hours later, once he'd returned

to the barn. He'd been doing a good deal of nothing in order not to return to the house. While he'd been expending energy on useless tasks, it had occurred to him his mistake had been letting Zoe think she had a right to stay with them during her visit. He should have packed her off that first night to a hotel.

"Daddy?"

"Hey, pumpkin."

Lydia hopped up onto a sawhorse and sat, swinging her legs. "Dinner will be ready soon. Mommy ran out for a loaf of bread."

"Mom's making dinner?"

"Yep. And we're baking cookies after."

"That's nice."

"Are you mad at Mommy?"

Luke crouched down, eyeing the line of a board he'd been sanding. To what purpose, he had no idea. "Sort of," he said.

Lydia said nothing, her gaze glued to him, feet in pink boots swinging back and forth. Luke glanced in her direction.

"What are we having for dinner?"

"Lasagna."

With a nod, Luke straightened up and returned

to sanding. "Mommy can't stay here. You understand that, right? We're not married anymore. If she's really going to stick around, she'll have to get an apartment in town and we can set up a schedule."

"A schedule?"

This was not something he should be discussing with his eight-year-old daughter. He knew that. Setting the sanding block down, he turned to face her. "I forgot my afterschool hug, didn't I?"

With a hop off the sawhorse, Lydia darted into his arms. He picked her up and snuggled her close, breathing in the cold air and shampoo fragrance of her hair. "What's the weather report say, kiddo?"

"I dunno. I didn't watch today. Do you think we'll be able to skate soon?"

"I think it's a sure bet by Christmas."

Lydia squealed right in his ear. He winced.

"Sorry, Dad. Will Allie skate with us?"

Luke didn't answer. He wasn't sure why his daughter asked the question. In all of this, he hadn't forgotten about Allie, not for a single minute, but he'd been trying not to think of her. Allie Roberts was a complication she'd never meant to be. He

missed her all the more because of that.

*   *   *

Allie fidgeted with the three photos on the counter. She'd tied ribbon through the holes punched in each but hadn't yet taken the time to climb into the window and hang them on the tree. This trio brought the total to twenty-two. Not exactly what she'd envisioned when she first put up the sign. Better than zero, she supposed. She could fill in the rest of the branches with the cinnamon sticks she'd originally brought in when Lydia was supposed to help her.

At the thought of Lydia, and subsequently Luke, Allie sighed. Todd looked up from his perusal of the hoagie he was deciding whether to eat. "Are you going to hang those up or what?"

"In a minute."

"Where's yours? You still haven't brought one in."

"I know," Allie said. "I will."

"When? Fourth of July?"

"Maybe." She jerked her chin at Todd's sandwich. "Eat that, will you? You know the lull doesn't usually last long."

## WINTER LIGHT

Marching out from behind the counter, she headed for the window. Once there, she clutched the three photos against her chest and watched the people passing by outside. She had half-expected Lydia would insist on bringing her mother in to the store, but Allie had seen neither hide nor hair of the ex Mrs. Luke and her daughter, or of Luke either. Several times Allie had been tempted to call him, but that seemed ridiculously needy and meddlesome. He needed this time. They all did.

Allie pulled over the stepstool and climbed into the window, taking care not to trample the artificial snow. She hung the photographs, making sure they faced outward, and paused before exiting to eye the skates leaning against the painted log. She hadn't put on those skates for several years. She suddenly hankered for the feeling of the blades beneath her feet as she sped across the ice. Luke had talked about that being their first real date, a night of skating. She had no idea if it would happen now. It might do her a world of good to make that date with herself.

A tap sounded on the window. Allie jerked around, her mind immediately going to Lydia Hollis. Instead she found the woman she'd been dreading, leggy and beautiful, silky hair long, eyes the color of smoke.

Zoe raised her hand in a hesitant wave, yelling through the glass. "Are you Allie?"

Heart pounding, Allie nodded.

"May I talk with you for a minute?"

"Sure. I'll be right out."

Allie didn't even bother with her jacket. She stood on the sidewalk with her arms wrapped around a sweater too thin for the weather, trying hard to keep her teeth from chattering.

"We weren't introduced the other night. I'm Zoe Hollis."

So, she still went by her married name. Allie grimaced, turning it into a smile before the woman noticed. "Allie Roberts." She shook Zoe's hand, withdrawing her fingers as soon as possible in order to tuck them back under her arm pit. Goodness, it was turning into a frigid evening.

"Don't you want to go inside?"

"I'm good."

"I wanted to thank you for helping out with Lydia these past few days."

Allie nodded. She hadn't really been helping out, but whatever.

"I…I realize I've failed Lydia the last couple of years. And Luke. But I'm back now."

Allie nodded again, more slowly, stomach churning

in anticipation of where the conversation was headed.

"Lydia seems fond of you. She's talked about you quite a bit. And yet...I don't...I want us to heal. I appreciate all you've done, but I think that healing would best take place without any distractions. You understand me, don't you?"

"I'm not sure that I do." Allie's teeth clacked together and she tightened her jaw. At this rate, she was going to come down with pneumonia.

"I think you should leave Luke and Lydia to me now. You should, well, go back to your own life."

"Huh." Allie arched her brows. "All right."

Without saying goodbye, Allie started back into the store, but paused at the door. She faced Zoe, who watched her with a peculiar expression. "That's all well and good," Allie said, "but no matter what else you may decide to do with your life, you have to stop treating your daughter as if she's disposable. She loves you, you know."

Allie spun and yanked open the door. She walked past Todd and Emma, barely sparing them a glance, and slipped inside the bathroom, closing the door quietly. Two seconds later there was a knock.

"Go away."

"Are you okay?" Todd. Good old Todd.

"Yeah. Just give me a minute. I'm trying not to throw up."

ROBIN MADERICH

*     *     *

Zoe had shouted from the front door five minutes ago that dinner was ready. Reluctant to leave the barn and Lydia's animated, one-sided conversation, Luke took his time. But he couldn't be rude. After securing the barn door, he grasped Lydia's hand in his and walked slowly across the hard-packed ground beneath the last light of evening, a blue like Lydia's eyes. Like his own. Zoe's were pale and striking, definitely the stuff of movie stars. And Allie's? Melted chocolate in candle light.

"What's so funny, Dad?"

"Just something I was thinking."

"Do you know how long Mommy is staying?"

"I don't, honey." As usual, Zoe hadn't made clear her plans. Perhaps she had none. Her spontaneity, her one-day-at-a-time attitude had endeared him when they first met. Not so much after Lydia's birth, and definitely not in the stretch of time leading up to their divorce.

"I hope she stays until Christmas."

If Zoe returned to California, free-spirited and neglectful of her daughter's needs, it would be a massive setback for Lydia. And yet he couldn't let Zoe blackmail him with that into taking her back. Sure, he wanted her in Lydia's life. Just not in his.

As he entered through the mudroom so he could

remove his dirty coat and boots, the smell of homemade sauce hit him. He inhaled, deeply. Zoe was doing her best to make it hard for him to turn her out. He wondered how badly things had gone for her in California. There had to be a reason she'd come back, something more than his conversation with her or hers with Lydia. Or was he being too harsh?

Lyddie preceded him into the kitchen. When Luke followed, he almost tripped over his stationary daughter. Lydia appeared transfixed by her mother, who stood in front of the stove slowly returning her phone to her pocket, her face shining with moisture from the heat of the oven, her silver-gray eyes alight. Zoe stared for a long moment at Lydia before raising her gaze to meet his.

"Luke, we have to talk."

"Yeah," he said. "We do."

*Chapter Ten*

Allie spun the papier-mâché reindeer one way and then the other on the table top. She'd made it oh-so-many-years ago when she'd been in an artsy phase, painting the lop-sided body a lovely shade of lavender, hooves and antlers a deep teal, with wires through the ears dangling silver jingle bells. A silly thing, but this had always signified Christmas to her. When she put the reindeer out, the season had begun.

Why she'd hadn't displayed it sooner she wasn't certain, but Todd's words as she left the store had galvanized her.

"Get off your ass, woman, and start celebrating Christmas. You don't need a man for that."

She laughed again in an attempt to lift her mood still further, and released the deer, taking a step back for a better view. The reindeer tumbled sideways and fell from the table. With a frown, she picked it up. Some damned critter had chewed the back hoof off.

Allie released a breath through her nose, reaching for a coaster. After positioning not one, but two coasters beneath the leg to make the reindeer level, she dropped onto the cushion of the couch, studying the boxes spread across the living room floor, all of them open and revealing fake greenery, glittery balls, snow globes, figurines. She looked at the glass of sparkling wine she'd poured herself, light reflecting in the tiny bubbles. With a decisive movement she stood, turned off the overhead fixture and climbed the stairs to bed.

In less than ten minutes, Allie was burrowed beneath the mounded quilt, lights off. The illuminated numbers on the alarm clock sent a green glow into the night. Quarter to eleven. She wouldn't have the energy to stay up for the eleven o'clock news again until the middle of January.

Awakening at what felt like the small hours of the night, Allie listened for the sound that had roused her from slumber. She didn't hear anything. The cottage was silent. Absolutely silent. Not even the hum of the refrigerator or the tick of hot water through the baseboard. Allie glanced at the clock, finding the face blank. She sat up and turned the light switch on the bedside lamp. Nothing. The chill of a cooling house danced along her arm.

Well, another blanket would keep her until morning. In a minute, she'd get up and retrieve a second comforter from the closet. For now, she could snuggle back into the leftover warmth trapped beneath the covers and enjoy the silence. She gave a brief thought to her parents in their home at the far side of the property—funny, how many families did that around Connor Falls, generations building on the same piece of land, staying close—until she recalled they'd gone to Florida. Back in time for New Year's, they'd promised cheerily. In the meantime, she was responsible for their house as well.

Allie pushed her arm back out into the cold and snatched her cell phone from the nightstand. Due to the frequency of outages, she had the electric company in her contacts and brought up their number,

the whirring ring the only sound in the night. After five of them, the automated message came on. Allie dutifully pushed the proper digits, first to report the outage and then to listen to the status. The outage, the voice told her, was due to weather conditions in her area. Weather conditions?

Allie leaped out of bed and ran to the window, where she pushed aside the curtains. Hard to see, but the tree nearest to the house appeared to be gleaming. Ice. Crap. Not one person who had come into the store had mentioned an ice storm on its way. Discovering the cell phone still in her hand, Allie turned it over to view the time. Three forty-five. No point in trying to go back to sleep. She'd normally be up for the day in little more than an hour anyway.

Dressing in her warmest clothes, Allie ticked off in her mind the things she needed to do. First, set all the faucets in the house to drip, just in case the outage and the frigid temperatures persisted long enough to freeze the pipes. Unplug most of the appliances to avoid a surge when the electricity came back on. Then she would head over to her folks' to do the same thing there. She'd start their generator to make sure it worked after two seasons of inactivity. Hopefully she wouldn't have to use it.

Having accomplished what she needed to in her

own home, she put fresh batteries in the flashlight and slipped it into the pocket of her ancient parka, followed by the keys to both houses and her cell. At the door, she pushed her feet into heavy-soled, waterproof boots for the trek across the fields. Until the sun came up and the roads were treated, she wouldn't be taking her car anywhere.

After locking the door behind her, she yanked on her gloves and reached out with one foot to test the surface of the porch steps. They were slick as a rink, the ice too thick to break up by stomping on it. She added another thing to her list: Ice Melt from her parents' garage. Traversing the steps and the slippery concrete pad at the base, Allie made it to the grass. Crunchy underfoot, the vegetation provided more stability for walking than any smoother surface. With a quick re-check of her pockets, she headed out into the night, freezing rain pelting her covered head and shoulders like thrown pebbles.

*   *   *

"Dad! Daddy! It's freezing in here!"

With a grumble, Luke rolled over. "Climb in, pumpkin." He flipped back the covers. Lydia dove into the bed beside him, preceded by a blast of chill

air. "Wow," he said, "it is cold. Did the heater stop working?"

"Dunno." Lydia burrowed against his side, pressing her face into the fabric of his T-shirt. Luke glanced toward the clock as he slid his arm around her.

"Did you knock the clock on the floor?"

"Nope. Where's Mommy? She's not on the couch."

"She went to a hotel. Don't you remember?"

"Right." Lydia became silent, digging her ice cube toes into his thigh through his pajama bottoms.

"It'll be all right, Lyddie. Didn't we talk about this?"

Lydia nodded against his ribs. The discussion with Zoe had been a tough one, but everything had to be said. Afterward, he'd spoken with Lydia about Zoe's move to a hotel room until she'd figured out what she was doing. The phone call Lydia had walked in on had been from Zoe's agent in California. He had expected her to race out the door for the very next flight, but she hadn't. Maybe she really had changed.

Luke squinted at the nightstand. He caught the vague, boxy shadow of the clock, but no numbers. The electric was off. Once upon a time, he'd kept a windup clock on the nightstand, too, but Lydia had laid claim to it one morning and he hadn't seen it since. He did, however, still have a watch and he pulled it close to check the time. He groaned.

"I've got to get up. I'll start a fire in the fireplace and you can sit in front of it when it's toasty."

"What's going on, Dad? Why is it so cold in here? And dark? Is the electric off again?"

"Yep," said Luke. "Afraid so." He pulled his jeans on over his sleep pants and shoved his bare feet into a pair of sneakers, then slipped into the sweatshirt jacket he yanked from the open closet. Heading through the house to the back door, he paused a moment to peer at the patio through the glass. Rain and sleet pummeled the frozen pavers, forming a vast, treacherous sheet of water-covered ice. On the far side, a tarp covered the split logs stacked against the garage wall. With a muttered expletive, he retraced his steps to the living room and grabbed the flashlight from the mantel. The supply of wood in the basket beside the hearth was minimal but would have to do for now. Rather than risk breaking his neck, he laid the small stack across the andirons and lit the kindling beneath. As soon as he had the flames leaping high, he rose from his knees and went in search of the radio.

Lydia appeared in the hallway, trailing the blanket from his bed around her shoulders and to the floor. She walked past him and went straight to the raised hearth where she sat, the blanket wrapped around her legs. "I looked out your window. It's pretty yucky out there. Do you think I'll have school?"

"As soon as I find the blasted radio, I'll let you know."

"Try the pantry. That's where you put it last time."

"The pantry. Right."

The cell phone rang. Luke snatched it off the dead charger and tucked it against his ear as he shined the flashlight inside the disorganized pantry. "Hello?"

"Luke, it's Frank. Where the hell did this crap come from?"

"I don't know. Last I heard was rain. You have electric?"

"It's flickered a few times, but its holding. Apparently the roads are hazardous. Beth's been called in early to work due to the accidents of the insane. I'm heading out to put the chains on now so I can get her there. I just wanted to let you know I'm not sure what time I'll make it to your place."

"Don't worry about it. I appreciate the call.

Hey, did you happen to hear what they're doing about school?"

"Two-hour delay, but it wouldn't surprise me if they call it for the day, soon."

"Thanks, Frank. Be safe, okay?"

"Yep, you too," said Frank, and hung up.

Luke set the phone on the counter and turned to face his daughter. She stared back at him, knees jumping in anticipation beneath the blanket. "Two hours, as of now. You can either curl up in front of the fire to sleep for a bit longer, or I can make us some oatmeal on the stove."

"Oatmeal!"

Strange kid, Luke thought with a smile. He removed a box of wooden matches from the drawer and lit the burner on the gas stove, preparing to make them both breakfast.

*　　*　　*

It had taken Allie a lot longer than she'd hoped to cross the fields to her parents' house, and the frozen precipitation hadn't let up. She felt chilled to the bone, her parka was saturated, and her feet had gone numb inside her boots. Once she got to the house, she couldn't hope for any respite, and she still had to go back to her own place after. She began to think she should have risked the car out on the road. At this rate, she'd end up with hypothermia.

Spotting a long, darkly shining strip in the landscape, she realized she'd reached the driveway. She walked in the grass alongside the glazed blacktop all the way to the garage, then went behind and chipped the ice from the doorknob in order to insert the key. Once inside, she crossed the garage to the interior door and unlocked that one as well. She shirked out of her parka as she stepped into the house where she and her brother had grown up. Compared to the outside, the temperature inside the kitchen felt downright balmy. She knew it wouldn't for long, though. Her best bet was to borrow a dry sweatshirt and socks from her mother's drawer before she did anything else.

Once she'd changed—adding a pair of sweatpants to the ensemble before throwing all her wet clothes over the shower curtain rod—Allie went to the living room. She hadn't planned to stay any longer than necessary, but wood had been laid in the hearth of the fireplace prior to her parents' departure for Florida. She couldn't find any kindling, so rolled up a couple of pages of newspaper and shoved them under the logs and lit them. Huddling close to what was, at best, a meager conflagration, Allie warmed her hands.

Maybe if she stuck around a while, the electricity would be restored and she wouldn't have to spend the day worrying about the water spigots she'd left open in the bathrooms and kitchen. Either that or the temperature would rise enough that freezing would no longer be a consideration. Then, the roads would merely be wet and she could drive her car into town without being white-knuckled or, worse, finding herself in a ditch somewhere.

Allie rose from the hearth as the logs caught. She put the screen in place and sat on the couch after pulling the afghan from the back of it. She spread the crocheted length over her legs and up to her shoulders, breathing in the scent of her mother's perfume trapped in the yarn. In the silence, she heard nothing but the crackling of the flames and the intermittent drip of water from the kitchen faucet. Soon that, too, would cease, as the pipes emptied.

Allie leaned her head back against the cushions

of the couch and closed her eyes, spending a few self-pitying moments thinking about Luke. She would have enjoyed getting to know him. For a little extra torture, she pictured running her fingers through his soft, dark hair.  He'd worn it shorter back in high school. She liked the way he wore it now. Lydia resembled him in coloration more than she did Zoe. Allie thought about that, too—the circumstances of Luke's breakup with his wife. Though the fault was likely the result of the sticky threads of two lives entwined and pulling apart, what Allie found bewildering was the fact Luke's ex-wife had left not only him, but their daughter. Not that it mattered now. Zoe was back and apparently planned to stay.

Well, there was no use crying over spilled milk, or whatever the stupid saying was.  While she was biding time in her parents' house, she ought to look through some of the photo albums and choose a memory of her own for the tree in the display window. She'd let it go long enough.  Todd was starting to lose patience.

Smiling at the thought of Todd at his wit's end, Allie pulled the albums from the shelf under the coffee table and set them on top. By flashlight and firelight, she started with the oldest, which began prior to her earliest memories here in this house. Soon, she came to baby pictures of herself and Jimmy, and birthday parties, and flipped through to find a photo of her first time on ice skates. Picking out one photo representative of a cherished memory was going to prove difficult and time-consuming. She should wrap the albums in a garbage bag as protection against the weather and take them home. Lugging them across the fields didn't seem prudent either, however. Perhaps after the store closed she could drive back and grab them.

Undecided and unwilling to venture back into the sleet and cold, Allie continued to peruse the old photos. She had to wait for the fire to die down, anyway. She certainly wouldn't leave the house until she was assured of that.

Outside, the weather seemed to be undergoing a change. Ice pellets rapped against window glass with increasing intensity. A rising wind howled across the chimney and echoed down the stones. Allie glanced aside at the flames and saw them shiver in the updraft. Last time she'd watched the weather report had been three days ago. How could something like this come up so unexpectedly?

Allie gathered up the albums and carried them to the kitchen counter, where she inserted them one by one into a plastic bag for retrieval later that night. Wind whistled through a gap in the kitchen window frame. She'd have to talk to Mom and Dad about that. If not mistaken, the wind had been making a shrill calling through that same breach since she was a kid.

With her thoughts on repairs and one hand on the bag of albums, Allie reached for her parka. It was her very last thought before the world exploded.

*Chapter Eleven*

"Are you worried, Dad?"

"About what, Lyddie?" Luke peered through the smear left by ice-crusted wiper blades across the windshield. He turned off the truck radio to aid in his concentration. The sound of tire chains crunching along the slick roadway distracted him enough.

"About Allie not answering her phone."

"No. Like I said, she probably forgot to charge it.

She'll be happy to see us, though. How will she get to work in this mess without a ride, right?"

"Right," Lydia agreed quietly.

Odd, how both he and Lydia had spoken Allie's name at the same time while sitting at the island eating their oatmeal. He couldn't even remember what he'd been about to say. He only knew that after her name had died in the air between them, leaving them staring at each other with spoons of congealing oatmeal gripped in their fingers, he had set his down and gone straight for his phone.

Receiving no answer from Allie, he'd calmly banked the fire and shut and secured the glass doors across the fire well, then told Lydia to get dressed, to bundle up. He blew out the candles, took Lydia's hand, headed out to the truck, stopping for the first aid kit on the way. Now why the hell had he done that?

His stomach churned, thinking of time lost as he'd put the chains on the pickup's tires. No choice, though, as he couldn't get anywhere on these roads without them.

Clutching his phone in her hand, Lydia looked down at the screen and directed him to take the next right. He cut off the expletive that flew to his tongue when he saw the incline. Downshifting, he felt the chains grind in. The truck crept up the hill, maintaining a slow but steady speed.

"According to this, Dad, there should be a driveway on the left soon."

"Okay, sweetie." Somewhere around ten minutes ago, he'd bitten down hard on the inside of his cheek. He could still taste blood.

Spotting the driveway, he steered onto gravel, making slow progress toward the front of a small cottage. Liberally coated in ice, Allie's car sat parked beside it. Luke stopped the truck, pulled up the parking brake.

"Stay here, Lyddie. I mean it. Stay right here and wait for me."

He climbed out and made his way to the front door. Shielding his eyes from the headlights of his pickup, he looked through the oval glass window. Nothing moved inside. Of course, she could be sound asleep, unaware of the weather. The house sounded too quiet for her to have electric. She'd be happy they hadn't let her oversleep. Yes, she'd be happy about that.

Lifting his fist, he pounded on the door. He couldn't rid himself of the overwhelming sense of urgency. Please Allie, he begged silently, just come down and answer the door.

Suddenly he felt a hand on his sleeve, tugging at his arm. Unclenching his fingers, he stared down at his daughter. "Lydia, didn't I tell you—"

"Daddy, look over there."

Luke turned his head to follow the direction of Lydia's pointing. He sucked in a sharp breath. Over the rise the clouds were being lit from below by a vicious orange glow.

"That isn't the sun, is it Dad."

*     *     *

"Hold on tight, Lyddie."

Forgoing a return to the road, Luke gripped the wheel tightly with both hands as he drove the truck straight across the fields, feeling the chains rip through frozen grass to the turf beneath. Directing Lydia to dial 9-1-1, he had her hold the phone up to his ear while he gave an approximate location to the dispatcher and told her something was on fire. The woman informed him they'd received a call from a neighbor, as well, and that fire trucks were on route, if not there already.

He didn't let up on the gas pedal. 'If not there already' wasn't good enough for him.

"What'd they say?"

"It's the Roberts' place. Allie's parents' house. It's on fire."

Lydia made a little squeak. Luke risked a glance at her. Moisture stood out along her lashes.

"Don't worry," he said. "Everything will be all right."

He didn't believe that for one minute.

*　　*　　*

Allie felt herself floating. She knew the sensation. It was familiar to her. Her arms stretched out to either side for balance. A beginner's trick. Her legs moved smoothly, though, her ankles not wobbling at all as she pushed off on one foot, then the other, on her brand new skates. After a moment she opened her eyes. Pristine and white, ice stretched as far as she could see beneath the pearly sky. The wind seared her face, making it sting. The sound of the wind, her blades, was muffled. Of course. She wore her new earmuffs over her ears, red plaid and lined with sheep's wool. She'd gotten them for Christmas. Before long, she felt as if she'd been skating forever, and leaped and spun, then tipped her head back, forming a deep arch in her spine as she circled, her arms like wings, her hands moving gracefully through the air. From above, winter light fell upon her, soft and luminous.

The air, the whispering breeze, began to call her name. She almost fell. Somehow, she managed to stay upright.

*I don't want to go home yet.*

She wanted to skate on and on forever. Alone and free. But she wasn't alone. She caught sight of two people, a man and a little girl, moving away from her. She called out to them, thinking she might know who they were, or they might know her, but they kept right on going, away across the ice.

"Stop! Stop!"

Her skate caught in an old track and she fell, hard. The winter light darkened around her.

*   *   *

Luke held Lydia's fingers tightly in his own. Silent and brave, she watched the medics load Allie into the ambulance. One of the EMT's came back over to them. He pointed at Luke's hand.

"You should get that checked out," he said. "Burns can be nasty."

Luke grunted. Lydia lifted her head to the medic. "Is Allie going to be okay?" she asked.

"She might have a concussion. She's still only semi-conscious. Her burns are minimal, all things considered. Don't think any bones are broken either, but they'll check your friend over at the hospital. Your dad did a good job, honey. Don't let any of the firefighters hear me say that, though. They don't like it when someone rushes into a burning building."

Luke closed his eyes, recalling the terror of the moment when he'd seen boot prints trailing up to the back door of a house from which flames were shooting into the sky, unimpeded by the spray of water from the fire hose. When he'd located her, Allie had been ice cold in his arms despite the searing heat of the fire. Dead. He'd been sure she was dead.

In his right arm, the one with the burned hand, he clutched a ragged, half-melted bag of photo albums. Allie had been holding them. From the look of the situation, these photos might be all her parents would have left of the contents of their home. The neighbor who'd called had told the dispatcher the Roberts were in Florida, thinking to be helpful, to protect the firemen from undue risk. No one had seen the prints shuffling across the icy grass.

Luke shifted the weight of the albums against his chest as he turned toward the truck parked at an angle in a patch of churned up mud. A single photo fluttered to the ground. Lydia bent and picked it up, holding it out to him. He took the photo, squinting at the image through the pelting rain.

In the fluffy white hat and thick cable sweater he remembered, a fourteen-year-old Allie performed a pirouette on the ice of his father's pond, right before nightfall. The sky behind her beautifully postured body glowed soft and gray. Luke turned the photo over, studying the familiar handwriting.

"Thought you might like this. R."

Rory had taken this photo. Luke had never known.

*　　*　　*

Once again, Allie thought she heard her name.

This time, however, the calling possessed substance, strong, distinctly male and persistent. The voice sounded like it might be at her ear. Annoying, like a baritone mosquito. She considered swatting it away and started to lift her hand, but she remembered her wrist had broken. Right there on the ice. After Luke had kissed her.

No. That was wrong. That was years ago.

"Allie."

She lifted the eyelid of one eye. The light was bright.

"Allie."

She let the lid drift downward again. Easier to take the darkness than the light. After a moment she felt a hand on hers. "Don't. It's broken."

"What?"

Right. Not broken. Where on earth was she? "Who is that?" she managed.

"Oh, hell, Allie. Don't you remember me?"

She forced her eyes open again, squinting through her lashes. A shadow moved, blocking the light of an overhead fixture, revealing a careworn, handsome face. Allie released her breath in a sigh.

"Of course I remember you," she said. "Luke Hollis, the man who's kissed me twice without a by-your-leave."

"Without a what?"

"A by-your—never mind. I'm in the hospital, aren't I? Can you help me sit up?"

She felt his arm snake beneath her back, lifting her. She reached behind and propped the pillow into place.

"Better?"

"Yes." She could see him now. He looked haggard and gray as he raised a bandaged hand and lowered it onto hers. "What happened to you?" she asked, gaze fixed on the white wrapping.

"Nothing major. A little burn, that's all."

"A little burn? How did you—oh."

Luke lowered himself onto the edge of the hospital bed, ducking his head to look her in the eye. He held his gaze on hers. Waiting.

Allie ground her teeth together, fighting back tears. "The house is gone, isn't it?"

"Yes, I think so."

She thought of that and all such devastation entailed. She needed to call her parents and Jimmy and let them know. She needed to get out of the hospital and back over there to see what could be salvaged, for Mom and Dad's sake. As she considered everything, her head began to ache. She looked up at Luke, who had straightened. Her brow twisted.

"Why were you there? I don't remember you coming with me. No, you didn't. I walked over in the storm alone. But you...you were there. You called me back. You and Lydia. Oh, God, where's Lydia?" She started to push off from the bed, but he took her hands and held her back.

"She's fine," he said quietly. "She's with her mother."

"But Lydia was there, too, right?"

"She was there, too. Yes."

"In the house?"

"No."

"You were in the house."

"Yes."

"Luke..."

"I came to see if you needed a ride to work and saw your parents' house on fire."

Allie frowned. She could tell he was leaving something out. "But how did you know? What would make you think to even go there? Luke, I don't understand."

Dropping his head forward, he shook it from

side to side. After a moment, he looked back up at her, blue eyes bright. "It doesn't matter, Allie. Please. I pulled you out. You're alive. That's all that matters, because I thought you weren't."

"But—"

"Enough," he said, a rumbling break in his tone. He cleared his throat. "No more talking."

She found herself in his arms in the time it took her to blink. His mouth lowered over hers in a careful, lengthy communion, and then he drew away.

"There," he whispered. "Without a by-your…what did you call it?"

"A by-your-leave. Permission, basically," she explained.

"Permission?"

She laughed, a weak sound even to her own ears. "But I was joking. You certainly don't need permission." Grabbing his collar, she pulled him close. "And neither do I."

*Chapter Twelve*

Allie poured the last bit of water from a former juice bottle into the dirt of the nearest poinsettia. That made fourteen floral get-wells—twelve poinsettia plants and two Christmas lilies. She hadn't realized she knew that many people well enough to receive a gift of good wishes from them, but here they were, with even more cards, filling her cottage with seasonal cheer. In the corner stood a small balsam with white lights affixed, courtesy of Luke and Lydia. Yesterday Allie had hung the contents of a box of multi-colored candy canes from the branches and a few glass balls, along with short lengths of bright red yarn tied into bows. Yep, she was getting mighty tired of staying home. Thank goodness the doctor had given her the go-ahead to return to work today. Christmas was right around the corner. Although Todd had stepped in quite efficiently, Allie was anxious to get back.

As Allie pulled on her boots, the phone rang.

"Mom, hi."

"Allison, sweetie, are you really going into work today? Your father and I—"

"Mom, I'm good. Really. You just relax at Aunt June's, okay? It's bad enough you had to cut short your time in Florida because I blew up your house." The words caught in her throat as she spoke them. She'd been told repeatedly it hadn't been her fault, how she'd been lucky the gas leak hadn't ignited sooner, catching her inside the house rather than standing by the garage. How fortunate no one else had been there. But her Mom and Dad's home, all their cherished possessions, were gone. Unable to shake the guilt, Allie had resorted to joking about it so she'd be permitted to take the blame.

"Allison Roberts, what is that tone I hear?"

"Nothing, Mom. I'm good. I just—"

"You are not good. You do realize if your father and I had been home, we would have done the same thing, lit a fire in the fireplace? But we probably would have been cuddled up on the couch staying warm when the fumes ignited. So we *all* have a lot to be grateful for. It's only things that are gone, not people."

Allie blinked back tears. "But your house, all those memories…"

"The house can be rebuilt. And the memories we still have. All of us."

Closing her eyes, Allie leaned her head against the cushioned sofa back. "Do we, Mom? Sometimes I feel like we don't."

For nearly a half minute, her mother remained mute. Allie peered out between her lashes at the contents of her living room. At one time, everything she'd placed about the room had held some meaning for her. Right now, despite the wonderful sentiment of the newest additions, the things she saw felt meaningless.

"Allie…"

The use of the diminutive she preferred brought more moisture to dot her lashes. "I'm okay, Mom. I

really am. I've got to get going, though, before I decide to play hooky again."

"Stay home, then. From what I hear, Todd's doing a great job."

"I want to go." Allie pushed up off the couch. She walked nearer to the mirror, leaning toward it, frowning at the multitude of tiny, healing cuts on her face from flying glass. Her hair had been singed a bit on the right side of her head, but with some careful clipping the damage was barely noticeable.

"Allison, you don't sound…yourself. And I'm not surprised, all things considered. Just worried."

Allie frowned at her reflection. "I am alive."

"Of course you are!"

"No, I mean that's a really wonderful thing."

"It is…"

Glancing at the room behind her, mirrored in the glass, Allie made a decision. "I want to have Christmas here. In my own place. I can start a tradition. New memories."

"Can we all fit in there, dear?"

"We can damn well try."

"Allie!"

"I mean it. If we have to take some of the furniture out of the living room, we will. Tell Aunt June to come and whichever of her kids and their kids are free."

"Honey, that's a lot of work."

Allie laughed, moved by the first bubbling of amusement since before the accident. "Tell everyone to bring a dish. How's that? Less work for everyone."

"I…okay."

"I've gotta go, though. I love you, Mom."

"I love you, too, sweetie."

Allie hung up the phone and grabbed her coat. She shoved her arms into the sleeves and pushed the zipper up to her chin, thinking her mother probably thought she'd lost her mind. And maybe she had. Maybe an experience like the one she'd had brought on small bouts of insanity. Fine. She'd take it and hope for the best.

Driving into town, Allie observed people hustling along the sidewalks, chins scrunched down into the collars of coats, scarves around faces, bright mittens on hands, woolen caps in place. Clouding breath filled the air beneath the dove gray sky. Her car had barely heated in the short trip and she shivered in her down jacket. Allie thought longingly of a frozen pond, any pond, but pictured in her mind that long ago night on the solid body of water where Luke had kissed her. She hadn't seen him since the day he'd picked her up from the hospital and the conversations she'd had

with him on the phone had been brief. Fun. Lively. But brief. Several times she'd heard Zoe in the background talking to Lydia before Luke stepped into another room to speak to Allie.

Despite his fervent kisses in the hospital, she still wasn't sure where she stood with him. She wasn't ready to ask, either.

Finding a space around the corner from the bookstore, Allie steered her car up to the curb, parked, and climbed out. Each meter along the sidewalk had been covered with a candy-cane striped bag. No fee during the last week before Christmas. She and the other shop owners had pushed for that, and won. At least for this year. Allie stood a few moments with her own chin tucked into her jacket's upturned collar, taking deep, protected breaths as she contemplated the walk to the store. She'd felt a little more energetic when she started out.

Avoiding the curious stares of passersby as she made her way toward Connor Falls Book Emporium, Allie considered her crazy offer of having Christmas at her tiny cottage this year. But really, wasn't it time to step up? She could do this. Hopefully her energy returned before the big day.

Nearing the storefront, she spied a handful of people talking and pointing at the display window.

Well, crap, had Todd forgotten to water the tree? She pictured browned needles littering the floor. Or had it fallen down?

"Hi," said Gina as Allie drew closer. "How are you feeling? Your Mom called to tell Todd you were on your way. What do you think?"

Allie followed Gina's extended finger and swallowed, hard, then attempted to speak. No voice came out. Someone had set a tiny, book-reader spotlight on the floor below the balsam, pointing up at branches sparkling with a lightly sprayed coating of artificial snow. From each branch tip hung a black and white photograph. More than Allie could believe. "How—"

"A couple of us got together and made some calls, and pushed the townspeople with signs in our own stores. It was all Luke's idea, really." Gina winked at her. "He wanted you to be surprised."

Biting her lip, Allie stepped nearer to the glass. Surprised was not the word. Several hundred photos shifted from side to side in a current of air, some appearing to have been recently taken, others depicting moments in time from years past, made obvious by the mode of dress, the furnishings glimpsed in the background. The townspeople's favorite memories of the season, displayed to share

with the little corner of the world known as Connor Falls. And at the top, in a place of prominence…

Allie raised her gloved fingertips to her mouth. "Where…where did he…"

She stared up at the photo of her on the pond, poised in an instant of grace she'd forgotten she possessed. Luke's brother Rory had taken the photograph, an eighteen-year-old man in possession of a sophisticated artistic eye. Taken it the same night Luke had kissed her, probably only minutes before.

"This is why," a deep voice said at her ear.

Allie turned to gape at Luke at her side, finding his handsome, serious face bent near to hers. "Why what?"

"Why I kissed you." His countenance creased into a smile. "And Gina lied. It wasn't all my idea. It was Lydia's. She wanted to surprise you. And there's more. Come inside."

Luke took her hand to lead her into the store. Gina gave her another wink as they passed by. "What are you doing here, Luke?" Allie asked. "How did you know I was coming in?"

"Your mom gave me a call to let me know you were on your way."

"*Mom* called you? I don't—"

"Yes, we've become quite friendly since your

accident." Luke laughed as he reached for the door and held it wide for her to enter. Allie stepped inside and stopped dead.

More photos hung from paperclips slipped into the crossbeams of the dropped ceiling. Enlargements from a copy machine these looked like, and all of them of Allie, her brother, their parents in years gone by: Christmases, summer picnics, carving Halloween pumpkins, swimming in the lake…

"Allison."

"Mom. Dad!" Allie rushed into their arms, holding them close.

"Really, Allie," her father said gruffly, "if you'd wanted us home for Christmas, you could have left the house intact and just asked."

Yeah, this was where she got her whacked sense of humor in times of trouble. Allie grinned at her dad through her tears. He jerked his head to the side. "Your friends are here, too. They want to welcome you back."

For the first time Allie noticed the store wasn't filled with customers, but with people she knew. Friends, shopkeepers, and yes, customers she recognized, all staring at her with wide smiles. A banner hung over the counter reading *Welcome Back, Boss*, Todd standing beneath it with a somewhat smug

expression on his tearful face. Although enlarged, Allie recognized his handwriting on the paper above his head. He pointed at it and at himself, on the chance she hadn't.

"Allie!"

Lydia pushed her way through the crowd, Zoe making a grasp for her hand and then letting her go. Allie crouched down, opening her arms. Lydia ran into them.

"So your daddy says this was all your idea."

Lydia nodded, face alight with joy. "It was."

No hedging, no demure denial. Allie laughed and hugged her. "Thank you. Where did you get all these pictures?"

Lydia glanced up at her father, who'd come to stand beside them. Allie rose, Lydia clutching her hand.

"You had a death grip on a melted garbage bag when I found you," Luke said. "It was filled with photo albums." He nodded toward a box wrapped in Christmas paper on the counter. "They're all in there, cleaned up a bit, as a gift for you and your family."

Allie released her grip on Lydia's hand and placed both of her own over her face, engaging in a bit of a meltdown behind her fingers. Words of sympathy and encouragement ran in tiny whispers among the people gathered. Allie smelled the evergreen scent lodged in Luke's coat as he came close and slipped an arm around her shoulder.

"And there's cake," he whispered.

"From Gina's bakery!" Lydia chimed in.

"There's no doubt," Allie said as she lowered her hands, "that this will be the best Christmas ever."

*　　*　　*

An hour later, following the departure of the crowd of people who'd come to wish Allie well, Zoe paused in front of her, Lydia's hat in her hand. "Thank you."

"For what?" Allie said, glancing aside at Lydia's animated conversation with Luke.

"For not pulling any punches with that 'disposable daughter' comment the night I came to talk to you. I've taken a job in New York. It's only a couple of hours away. We've worked out a custody schedule, Luke and I. I won't abandon Lydia again. I won't abandon either one of them. No." This, as Allie opened her mouth to speak. "Not what you think. Luke's a good father. There's no reason he has to do it alone though. Our daughter has two parents. We need to act like it, even if we're not together as a unit."

Zoe turned her head and called Lydia's name. She held the hat out to her daughter as Lydia skipped over. "Put this on, peanut. It's cold outside." She turned back to Allie. "Lydia's going with me to my hotel. We're going to have dinner and watch movies and eat popcorn in bed. I believe Luke has plans. With you."

*   *   *

The sun moved toward setting, a pale lozenge nearly invisible behind the cover of soft, gray clouds. The world was without shadow, silver and brown and green, the ice on the pond as smooth as opaque glass. Crouched on his knees, Luke helped Allie to put on the painted skates he'd removed from the window display. He tied the new laces, touched the blades' edges, freshly sharpened. He rose and held out his hand. Allie slipped her fingers into his.

"You get tired, you just let me know."

She smiled at him, lips closed, her chocolate-syrup eyes luminous. "I'll be fine."

He clutched her hand until he was sure she'd gotten her legs under her properly, and then he let go, watching her skate across the ice, sure and strong despite her recent trauma. Must be like riding a bike.

Something you never forgot.

After a moment he followed, keeping his distance, his gaze glued to the elegance of her form, the confidence of her movements, the beauty that had so thrilled him all those years ago. He would kiss her again because of it, but not right now. Right now, he wanted only to watch her fly.

"Allie."

She turned, grinning at him, skating backward, her cinnamon hair blowing in wisps around her face. "Luke Hollis, I think I'm falling for you."

He skated a little nearer, so she could hear him better. "Ditto, Allie Roberts. But please don't mean that literally. No broken wrist this time around."

"No broken anything," she said, and with a laugh that rang across the ice she performed a perfect pirouette beneath the winter sky.

Titles in the Connor Falls Christmas Series:

*Hurry Home for Christmas*
Connor Falls Christmas Book One

*I Knew in a Moment*
Connor Falls Christmas Book Two

*Winter Light*
A Connor Falls Christmas Novella

*Light the Heart Home*
A Connor Falls Christmas Novella

*Home for the Holidays*
A Connor Falls Christmas Novella

*When the Heart Brings You Home*
A Connor Falls Christmas Collection containing
*Winter Light, Light the Heart Home* and *Home for the Holidays* in one volume